1 MONTH OF
FREE
READING

at

www.ForgottenBooks.com

By purchasing this book you are eligible for one month membership to ForgottenBooks.com, giving you unlimited access to our entire collection of over 700,000 titles via our web site and mobile apps.

To claim your free month visit:

www.forgottenbooks.com/free241259

ISBN 978-0-483-57062-7
PIBN 10241259

WHEN WE WERE WEE

THE MACMILLAN COMPANY
NEW YORK · BOSTON · CHICAGO
DALLAS · SAN FRANCISCO

MACMILLAN & CO., LIMITED
LONDON . BOMBAY · CALCUTTA
MELBOURNE

THE MACMILLAN CO. OF CANADA, LTD.

EVERYCHILD'S SERIES

WHEN WE WERE WEE

TALES OF THE TEN GRANDCHILDREN

BY

MARTHA YOUNG

AUTHOR OF "PLANTATION SONGS," "PLANTATION
BIRD LEGENDS," "SOMEBODY'S LITTLE GIRL,"
AND OTHER BOOKS

ILLUSTRATED BY PHOTOGRAPHS OF CIVIL WAR TIMES
AND BY DRAWINGS BY SOPHIE SCHNEIDER

New York
THE MACMILLAN COMPANY
1912

All rights reserved

TO

GESSNER

TO

WILLIE

AND ALL THE DEAR GRANDCHILDREN

WHO PLAYED SO HAPPILY IN

OLD GREENE SPRINGS

GARDEN

CONTENTS

WHEN WE WERE WEE

CHAPTER I

GRANDMOTHER'S WEDDING GLOVES

OUR Grandmother sat in her arm-chair with the round pillow in the back of her chair, her feet on a footstool, and her own black maid, Dilsey, holding an old brass-bound "small-box" for Grandmother to look over. Queer old things that had been in the brass-bound "small-box" were scattered about, and a pair of old white kid gloves, taken from the "small-box," lay in Grandmother's lap.

"These were my wedding gloves," said our Grandmother.

Then she told us what a long, long way those gloves had come by land, by water, by caravan, before they had reached her home of the long ago; for when on her wedding day Grandmother wore those gloves Alabama was not

yet a state of the Union, and things in those
days travelled in a slow way, as travel slowly
they must in a pioneer country.

And now it was War-time. Alabama was
again not a state of the Union, for our Grandfather had signed the Order of Secession at
Montgomery, and every one of our fathers
was in the army.

There were ten of us grandchildren, and we
thought it great fun to be all together at
Grandmother's house.

We did not expect to be long together, if we
thought of it at all, because at first we had
heard all the grown folks say: "At most the
War can last but six months."

But would you believe it! The War had
lasted already almost two years now! This
was our second War-Christmas.

No toys had run the blockade in a long,
long time, and we "little pitchers with long
ears" — how angry we children grew when
Aunts called us that! — had heard the grown

folks say to each other that we might have to
do without Christmas this year. Think of
that! Do without Christmas! Now we
knew that war was indeed a dreadful thing. —
To do without Christmas!

No grandchild had ever before heard of such
a thing. No Christmas! That very day, —
and it was Christmas Eve, too, — as we sat
listening, all ten of us, to Grandmother as she
told of the grand wedding and the white
gloves, we heard Aunts say to each other:
"There will be no Christmas this year."

The two Aunts sat at a window in Grandmother's room, and we distinctly heard them
say: "There will be no Christmas this year."

We grandchildren looked one at another,
one at another, one at another, until we had
all ten looked at all the others.

We knew now what war meant.

The two Aunts had said: "There will be
no Christmas this year."

"Come!" said Grandmother. It did not

matter to Grandmother how great and grown Aunts were; she said "Come!" to Aunts whenever it suited her to do so, just as our mothers said "Come" to us when we were naughty.

"Come, come!" said Grandmother. "No Christmas! I never heard of such a thing. It is bound to come, for it is down in the almanac."

Then one little grandchild, one who looked so solemn all the time that we thought he would make a great man some day, asked: "Grandmother, did Christmas stay away before when Alabama was not a state in the Union?"

We all thought it very smart of our "Judge" to ask that, and our Grandmother answered: "Never."

Then we all felt much better about Christmas!

Grandmother said again to the two Aunts: "Come, come! I would make Christmas out of these old gloves rather than not have Christmas come at all!"

Then Grandmother said to her own black maid Dilsey: "Dilsey."

Dilsey said: "Yas, ma'am."

Grandmother said: "Dilsey, put down the 'small-box' and go to the closet on the left of the fireplace and get out the bow-basket and bring it to me."

Dilsey said: "Yas, ma'am."

Dilsey put down the brass-bound "small-box," which all that time she had been holding for Grandmother to look over, and opened the closet on the left of the fireplace and lifted the bow-basket from a shelf and said: "Mistis, mus' I bring what's in it too?"

We looked at one another all around, and as we looked we wondered: "What is in the bow-basket?"

But in a minute we knew — every one of us — what was in the bow-basket, for the whole room was sweet with the odor of apples!

Then Grandmother put her two little wrinkled white hands into the bow-basket and took out two round, red apples; then she put her hands into the bow-basket again and took out two more round, red apples; five times she put her two hands into the bow-basket, and each time took out two round, red apples, for there were ten of us grand-children.

She did not say a word, and we did not say a word.

Dilsey, when she was told, put the bow-basket back on the shelf and came again to Grandmother's chair and took up the brass-bound "small-box."

Then Grandmother said to the oldest grand-child: "Take this apple, and eat it, and bring every seed out of it to me."

Then Grandmother said to the next oldest grandchild: "Take this apple, eat it, and bring every seed out of it to me."

Grandmother gave us each, one by one, all

ten of us, an apple, and to every one of us, one by one, she said as she gave it: "Take this apple, eat it, and bring every seed out of it to me."

Then we went out of Grandmother's room, all ten of us in a row, and we went down the path that ran by the camellia-japonica hedge, and there we sat down all in a row.

Then the oldest grandchild of all said: "Didn't Grandmother say that to us very solemnly?"

Then the next oldest grandchild said: "I felt so strangely as she said it!"

Then the next oldest said: "But there is nothing for us to do but to eat the apples."

So we sat all in a row, all ten of us, and began to eat the apples.

We were talking of many things, — there were always many things to talk of! — and we had eaten our apples almost down to the cores when the oldest grandchild of all cried: "Oh, the seeds!"

Then the next oldest of all the grandchildren cried: "Don't forget the seeds!"

Then "Judge," who had eaten farther down in his apple than any of us, said: "I am saving mine."

And he held up a magnolia leaf turned upside-down, and there on the soft brown lining of the leaf were laid two apple seeds, and Judge was eating down to the others.

So all ten of us picked up magnolia leaves and turned them upside-down and put apple seeds on them.

When all the apples were eaten, and the seeds of all saved, we found that one of us had six seeds, another five, others even eight or more. Then we talked a long time about the best way to carry to Grandmother the seeds that she had told us to bring back to her.

At length we decided to go in a row, all ten of us, carrying the apple seeds carefully on the magnolia leaves as if on trays, — "jade-trays,"

the oldest grandchild said, — and we decided to say, one by one, beginning with the youngest: "Thank you, Grandma. We enjoyed the apples very much, and here are the seeds you told us to bring you."

So we went in a row, all ten of us, one by one, and, beginning with the youngest, we said, one after the other, the very words we had planned to say.

Then Grandmother took the first magnolia leaf with the seeds on it that was handed to her, and she wrote on the brown lining of the leaf: "Ted."

Then on the brown lining of the next leaf she wrote also with the point of her knitting-needle: "Amaryllis."

Upon the brown lining of every leaf she wrote with the point of her knitting-needle the name of the grandchild who had brought the leaf.

Then she said: "Run away now! Every one of you ten grandchildren! Run to the rose garden to play. And don't let me hear of you again to-day!"

And we went.

The next morning — early, *early*, EARLY — for it was Christmas morning, just after stocking-opening time, Dilsey, Grandmother's own black maid, went to every room in the house where a little girl or a little boy slept. Dilsey knocked at every door of every room where a child slept, and she handed in a little, tiny white box.

At every door to which Dilsey went she said, just outside the door, when it was opened to her knock, just as Grandmother had told her to say: "A Merry Christmas to you from Grandma!" And Dilsey added every time of her own fancy: "Dat what Ole Miss say."

When every little girl and when every little boy opened the tiny box that Dilsey had handed in, there was, in each tiny box, a small white card. And on the small white card was a tiny white bag of meal (or what looked like a tiny bag of meal).

And there were on the cards mice! Tiny, tiny, tiny brown mice, running over the cards and up the bags of meal! Or what seemed to be tiny brown mice running after the meal-bags.

When a little later we all came together in the hall, all ten of us grandchildren, to show one another our early morning Christmas boxes, we found that one had five mice, another had six mice, and another had even as many as eight mice on the white cards, running after the small meal-bags.

Then suddenly Judge remembered that he had had just six seeds from his apple. Then one by one we remembered, until all of us remembered how many apple seeds we had had — and then we knew that the apple seeds had turned into little brown mice!

Yes, these were the apple seeds that Grandmother had told us to bring back to her.

Those funny little mice all had little whiskers

of black silk thread on their little pointed noses. Those little mice all had tails of black silk thread. They all had tiny legs of black silk thread stitches, which fastened them to the white cards.

We looked at those little mice and those little bags of meal, and we talked about them at times all Christmas day. They were so interesting and so queer.

But we could not guess what the bags were made of until at last the oldest grandchild of all cried: "Grandmother's wedding gloves!"

Then we knew.

The ten little bags were the ten finger and thumb-tips of the wedding gloves. The tips were turned wrong-side-out, and that gave them the soft, almost downy, look that bags full of meal have, and they were stuffed, those tiny bags, with perfumed cotton.

So our Grandmother, who always did what she said she would do, had indeed made Christmas out of her wedding gloves.

CHAPTER II

MOTHER'S GOLD THIMBLE

Doc and Amy and Elise and Willy-boy were in great trouble. Doc and Amy and Elise and Willy-boy all sat on the shady side of the woodhouse in the back yard and talked their troubles over.

They sat under the Palma Christi stalks that grew tall, taller than the woodhouse, and the shadows of the great leaves of the plant fell upon them like shadows of stars. Doc and Amy and Elise and Willy-boy were always fond of going to this favorite place of Doc's and watching the shadows of the leaves falling like black stars in the sunlight; but they all were in too much trouble to-day to look at the star shadows on the ground.

"I remember," said Doc, "that when the Pierret children from the next plantation

14

were here I got It from Mother to play with.
I don't remember any more."

"I remember," said Amy; "I don't know
exactly when it was, that I got It from Mother
to draw scallops on the apron that Aunts are
showing me how to buttonhole-edge for
Mother's birthday present. I remember that
the wounded soldier came just then, — and
I don't remember any more."

"I found your scalloping under the lilacs
where Toto had carried it, and though Toto
is such a mischievous dog, he hadn't torn it a
bit," said Elise. "A great deal has happened
to-day," she added; "we have had company
of our own — and the wounded soldier."

But even the thought of so eventful a day
could only divert their minds for a moment
from their great trouble. Doc, Amy, and
Elise and Willy-boy all shook their heads
solemnly as their thoughts went back to it.

"I remember," said Elise, and she hung
her head; "but I can't remember whether it

was to-day or yesterday, that I was so distressed at losing my little gold chain, my Christmas-before-the-War-chain, that I took It from Mother's basket and I went to the gravel walk where I last remembered wearing the chain, and I shut my eyes tight and I turned around and around, and I said : —

> 'Gold, find gold !
> What I have let me hold.
> Gold, gold, find gold !'

Then I threw It as far as I could with my eyes shut *tight!*   And sure enough when I opened my eyes there on the gravel lay my little chain near where It had fallen.   I was so glad to find my chain that I remember I ran and picked that up, — but whether I picked It up — I can't remember —"

At that Doc, Amy, Elise, and Willy-boy all looked more solemn than ever.

"And so I know," said Elise, "that I have been the worst of all !"

"I 'member," confessed Willy-boy, "that one day, maybe this day, I played I was cook-boy, and I was in the kitchen with Aunt Chloe, and I got It from Mother to cut teeny weeny biscuits with It; I don't 'member any more."

"We have all done wrong," said Doc, after a solemn pause.

Doc had a right to say that. He was the oldest. He was quite ten. Mother and Father both relied on him, and called him just "Son." Amy, Elise, and Willy-boy all said: "Yes, we have done wrong."

All the ladies in the neighborhood had met to sew for the soldiers, and Mother's gold thimble was lost. "We must all do something," said Doc, "to show that we are sorry we have been careless and to show that we will not be careless with Mother's gold thimble again."

"I saw a thimble case at the Ladies' Bazaar," said Elise; "it was made of a white walnut shell."

"Oh," said Amy, "that sounds as if we could make one — perhaps —"

"A walnut shell?" asked Doc.

"That is what she said," said Willy-boy.

"I think I can tell exactly how it was made," said Elise, who was as anxious as could be that something should be done.

"Don't let Mother know until it is finished," said Doc. "Then let us all look and look until we find the thimble, and then let us never lose it again."

" — If we can help it," said Amy.

"I will go and ask Aunts for a walnut," said Elise.

"Everybody must do something in the making of it," said Doc.

"Doc, I will tell you what will be your part," said Elise, who was the one who could tell how it was to be made. "You must cut the shell carefully open down the *seam* of it to divide the two halves, and then at the top and bottom of each shell a small hole must be made,—teeny tiny holes through which ribbons may be run."

"Yes," said Doc; "I can do those things. I can make the tiny holes by burning with a very hot wire."

"I will get a knitting-needle from Aunts," said Amy; "you can burn the holes with that."

"And what can I do?" asked Amy.

"There must be a wee silk bag to fit between the shells."

"Oh, I can make the wee silk bag," said Amy.

"And what can I do?" said Willy-boy.

"Somebody must eat the nut," said Elise; "Willy-boy, you can eat the nut."

When all were ready, Doc divided the nut carefully down the seam. Willy-boy ate the kernel, Doc scraped the inside of the halves of the shell until the inside was almost as smooth as the outside. Amy cut a bit from the end of her rose-colored sash, her prettiest sash, and, while she made the bag carefully to fit between the two halves of the shell, Doc and Elise went to heat the point of the knitting-needle that they might burn the holes. Oh, that was delicate work! The children had to be so careful not to crack the shells while the hole was bored in the top of each half-shell and another hole in the bottom of each half-shell. When the four holes were burned in — and not a crack in the shells — the tiny silk bag was finished too. Then some help from Aunts was needed, for the bag had to be fastened to the bottom of the half shells by running a very narrow pink ribbon through the two tiny holes. Then drawribbons had to be put in the top of the bag, and these, too, must be run through the holes in the top of the half-shells. At the top and bottom the ribbons were tied in pretty bowknots, while the two halves of the shell lay closely together, and the silk bag was hidden inside.

The thimble case was finished.

Thanks to the skill of Aunts, it opened and shut most beautifully on the draw-ribbons.

When the four children all went to hunt for the thimble, where do you think it was found?

Kitty-grey was playing with it in the corner of Mother's room, tossing it about on her forepaws. So the thimble was soon put into the new case.

"If we could only go to Mother right now!" said Elise.

But Mother was in the long parlor, sewing for the soldiers with the ladies of the neighborhood. For such important sewing she was using her silver thimble, for she thought that the gold thimble was lost.

"Now," said Doc, as the children waited for the time to pass and for the ladies to go; "when grown people are banded together to do anything, they call themselves a society and make a name for themselves."

"Yes," said Amy; "let us do that. That

will be fine. We are banded together not to lose Mother's thimble any more, — if we did lose it this time, — anyhow, we are a society for that now, and we must make a name for ourselves —"

"Oh, that sounds exciting," cried Elise. "I have heard the soldiers, specially the Lieutenant and the Captain, say they wanted to make a name for themselves in battle. — Let us be the Company of Trusty Thimblers!"

Elise was always good at making names. I think if she had been a soldier she would have made a name for herself right away!

"We are the Trusty Thimblers!" said Doc, Amy, Elise, and Willy-boy all together.

So, as the last of the ladies of the neighborhood left, the Trusty Thimblers went hand in hand to Mother, and Willy-boy, at the end of the row of four, carried the thimble case because he was the youngest; and though he was the youngest, he had helped, too, for he had eaten the nut.

Wasn't Mother surprised with the gift of the thimble case! Wasn't Mother *pleased* with the gift of the thimble case!

Then Mother said that she wished never, never to lose that gold thimble because our Black Mammy had given each one of us, when we were wee, wee babies, our *first* drink of water from that thimble, because Mammy said that to insure beauty and long life and happiness and all good things to a child, its *first* drink of water must be from a vessel of gold, and we had no vessels of gold in our house, only many of silver — then. So Mammy had improvised a drinking vessel from Mother's gold thimble. Mother told  us that as she tied the thimble in its new case.

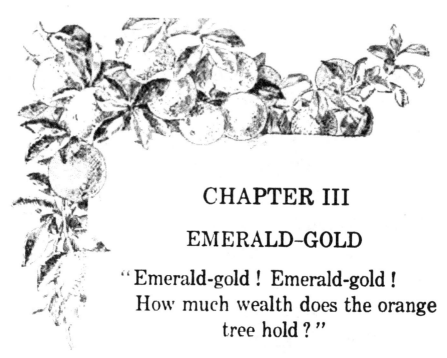

CHAPTER III

EMERALD-GOLD

"Emerald-gold ! Emerald-gold !
How much wealth does the orange
tree hold ? "

THAT was the song that Elise made about the orange-tree in our grandmother's front yard. Amy said that it was a beautiful song. Doc said that he thought so, too, — "as far as it went."

"Well," said Elise, skipping about very happily under the trees, "that grew in my head just as it is; and if any more grows, why, I'll tell you that, too."

"There might be something about pearls," said Amy; "for the white buds and blossoms are something like clusters of pearls."

24

"Yes, they are," said Elise.

"But," said Doc, "it is Elise's song, and it is only fair for us to let it alone until, as she says, some more of it grows in her head."

"Oh," said Elise; "I don't care how it grows if only it does grow; but anyway I am going right now to pick the ripest orange that I can see and make something pretty that Aunts showed me last week when I had a cold and had to stay in the house all day."

"I know how to make something, too," cried Amy, "but it is something that we all know."

"Let's each make something from an orange," suggested Doc, "and then let's all come together and show what we have made."

"And give a prize?" asked Em.

"Yes, a prize," consented Amy, whose word always weighed with us; "a cluster of blooms will be the prize for the best thing made of an orange."

So we all set to work making things, that is, all who were then at play in the yard.

Elise took her orange, the very nicest that she could reach on the tree, to the honeysuckle arbor to make the pretty thing that Aunts had made for her when she was ill. First she had to go into the house to borrow Mother's small penknife.

Doc went to his favorite workshop place, the shaded side of the woodhouse, where the rank growth of Palma Christi trees threw black shadow-stars from their leaves. He sat there a while to think and to remember what he had ever seen or heard of that could be made of oranges. He said afterward, when we all came together, that what he did make was easy enough, only he lost so much time in thinking and remembering; but then he did not have to go after a knife, — he had one in his pocket. That is the good of being a boy, a boy big enough to have two pockets, with a knife in one of them, — one always has a good tool at hand.

Amy sat down where she was, under the

orange-tree, to try to think of something to make that would be new to all of us; and while she thought, she ate three oranges.

Willy-boy sat down under the tree, too, and set to thinking with his chin in his hand and his elbow on his knee; but he kept saying that he could think of nothing, and he asked Amy if she could not divide her thinking with him.

Amy said: "Willy-boy, I haven't thought of anything either; if I had I would divide. But suppose you go and ask Mother to help you; you know when little boys are only three they have a right to Mother's help, even when there are prizes."

So Willy-boy went to ask Mother.

He came back directly, laughing and clapping his hands.

Amy said: "Mother helped you, didn't she?"

Willy-boy said: "Yes, she did."

Willy-boy asked Amy to pick him five even-sized, nice big ripe oranges, and with the

five oranges in his apron, held up tight and
fast, he ran back to Mother.

Elise was the first one ready with her "try-
for-the-prize"; but then, as she said, that was
natural, as she had known beforehand just
what she would make, while the others had to
think, to remember, or perhaps even to invent,
and so, of course, needed time. So Elise
waited quite patiently until the others were
ready. When the other four were ready, they
all came to the tree.

Willy-boy came, but he said that Mother
had told him to come back a little later for
his "try-for-the-prize." So, he stood smiling
under the tree with his arms folded and
looked at the others' "pretty things made of
oranges."

Elise showed hers first. It was an orange,
half peeled from the stem end, the peel being
divided into many small and even sections, and
each small, even section of the peel was turned
over and slipped under where the peel still

held to the orange, making many little loops of yellow peel all lined with white, and these looked like the curled petals of a large flower, while the orange itself made the rich center of the flower.

"Now," said Elise, who always saw things in a way of her own, "it is as if the orange had grown to be a flower again, only this time it is like a flower of gold instead of a flower of pearl; and," said Elise, "it looks to me something like a yellow lily."

"Yes, it does," said Amy; "and it is beautiful."

Then Doc asked us to excuse him if he turned his back on all of us. And when he faced us again he looked for all the world like an ogre! That was what Amy said he looked like, and we knew that Amy knew.

He had cut two rows of teeth out of the peel of an orange and had slipped them over his own teeth, and he looked fierce enough to frighten anybody! We laughed and we laughed.

Then it was Amy's turn, and she said that she had eaten three oranges — very slowly — and yet she had been able to think only of the way she and Elise had long ago made hats for dolls out of the half of an orange-peel, turning it up all around the edge, making a rim of white to a hat of gold, and then trimming the hat with a bunch of orange blossoms.

Elise said she was so glad that Amy had made one of those hats, because she always did love those orange-peel hats for dolls!

When it was Em's turn, she said she had thought of something a little new. She had a brood of tiny white chickens with green legs. The chicks were made of orange seeds with tiny bits of green thorn stuck in for the legs. She had cut a wing on either side of the seed by slicing it up half way, the point of the seed made the bill, and Em had dotted an eye with ink on each side of the bill.

Doc said that it was a new idea to make chicks out of orange seeds. He stood one of the chicks up in a piece of peel that looked like a small tray, and said that it reminded him of a song that old black Aunt Drusilla sang to put the smaller grandchildren to sleep : —

"Chicken in the bread-tray,
Scratching up dough!
Granny will your dog bite?
No, child, no!"

Willy-boy had become so much interested in looking at all the "try-for-the-prizes" that he forgot to go back for his own till Mother came to the edge of the gallery and called to him. Beside Mother stood her black maid, Mitty. Mitty held a small silver tray. A napkin was over the tray, and none of us, not even Willy-boy himself, knew what was under the napkin. Willy-boy ran to the gallery, and he came back to the tree, walking beside Mitty, just as eager as the rest of us to know what was under the napkin.

When he lifted the napkin, there on the tray were five little golden baskets. Each basket was made of the half of an orange-peel, and a strip of peel was left for the handle to the basket; a tiny bow of orange-colored ribbon was tied on the tip of the handle of each basket. We all cried out with delight at the beauty of those baskets, and we all told Willy-boy that his orange-toy was the best of all!

In the baskets was — ambrosia!

Ambrosia is made of bits of orange and grated cocoanut in equal parts, with sugar — much sugar! — and orange juice poured over all, with a taste of lemon juice in it, too.

Oh, how we all liked ambrosia!

We seated ourselves in a circle under the orange-tree and ate the ambrosia from the gold-colored baskets, and we voted one and all that Willy-boy should have the prize.

So Doc climbed the tree and plucked the most beautiful cluster of blossoms that he could find, for the blooms were rare when the oranges were ripening so fast. Amy reached up, because she was the tallest of us all, and took the cluster from Doc's hand, as he handed it down from the branch of the tree, so that it might not have a shattering fall, and she put the cluster of blooms into Willy-boy's hand.

Willy-boy said that he would give it to Mother, for it was Mother's thought that won the prize, and Mother's thought was the best of all; and he ran into the house with the blossoms.

Mother put the cluster in fresh water in a little vase on her work table, with the pretty shining let-me-up-and-down leaves and drawers, and she said she would look at it many times as she sewed. Ladies sewed all day long in those times for the soldiers, because the soldiers were our own.

CHAPTER IV

A PEACH-TREE AND A TINY BASKET

EM stood in the sunlight on the steps of the side gallery with two luscious peaches, one in each hand; and she called to the two boys who were playing in the yard beyond: "I have something for you, — both of you!"

Then the two boys ran a race to see which would get there first, and, after all, they both got there at the same time! So Em held her hands behind her and said: "Which hand, Judge?" You see, Judge did so much thinking that we felt obliged to call him by a serious name, although he had a very good name of his own.

Then Em said: "Which hand, Doc?"

Doc had a very good name of his own, too; but I never knew a family of brothers or cousins who did not have among them a Doc. You see it was always expected that one of the family would become a great doctor some day.

Judge chose one hand. I forget whether it was the right or left that day, and Doc, of

DOC AND JUDGE

course, took the other, as there were only two hands to choose from. It made no difference, however, because Em said that the peaches were exactly even, evenly ripe, evenly beautiful.

Peaches were no rarity at Grandmother's, for the orchard of peach-trees that climbed the gravelly hill in front of the house spread over nearly five acres. But these peaches were particularly fine, and they were from the first basket gathered from the tree Grandfather had planted with his own hands. So it was very kind of Em to choose two for those two boys, and she looked so dear standing there in the sunlight, with her hands behind her, asking "Which hand?" that somehow the giving of those peaches seemed to both boys an event.

Events were always made memorable in some way. There were the pressed bay leaves, still kept in the big black and gold Bible in memory of a great event, for those bay leaves had been used to decorate the old State House at Cahaba, when that town

had been the capital of Alabama. Then our
great-aunts, with other little girls, had strewn
flowers before the great French general,
Lafayette, when he had visited Alabama.
There was the quaint gold snuffbox, brought
from England, which made memorable to
us the friendship between our ancestor who
first chose America for his home and the
great orator, Fox. And so on ran the stories
of the many memorable things treasured in
Grandmother's house, down to the memorable
things of our own day; the bright brass but-
tons of the gray uniforms and the brass belt
buckles with the glistening "C-S-A" upon
them. Grandmother said that these would
be most famous some day, some distant
day, like the relics of the Revolutionary
War and other things, even older, that we
now treasured.

We found it hard to understand why these
things should be memorable, for these belts
and buckles, these trappings of war, we saw all

the time, and they naturally seemed ordinary, everyday things to us.

Indeed, only the oldest of us grandchildren (there were ten of us) could remember seeing our fathers and uncles in anything but war clothes, for the War had been going on several years now, and — but I started to tell how Doc and Judge wished to make memorable the event of Em's giving them the beautiful peaches.

The two boys sat on the heap of logs in the pasture for a long time, talking over what they could do to celebrate the event. At last Judge got up, saying he had an idea, and that he was going off to do the thing that he had thought of.

Doc could not think at all that day, it seemed to him, and he sat there on the logs in the blazing sun, until his sister Elise came to tell him that the children's dinner table was ready. She said: "What *are* you thinking about out here in this sun?"

Doc told her what was the trouble; he was not thinking, he was trying to think, but he was not able to think of anything. As they went to the house together he told Elise all about the two peaches, and how he and Judge wanted to make the gift memorable.

Elise did not seem to think the matter of any importance at all, and went skipping and jumping along beside Doc.

But just as they reached the house she said: "I tell you, Doc, — plant the kernel."

"There," said Doc; "I never thought of that."

"That is old, but somehow it seems new," said Elise; "just give a planting and invite us all, and then build a small pen around the place where you plant it, and, if it lives, call it Em's tree."

"I'll do it," said Doc; "I wonder what Judge will do? He had a thought."

So Doc invited all the children at children's table to come out to the planting of Em's tree in the southwest corner of Grandmother's orchard; and we all went.

The next oldest grandchild, the one who was always poring over a book, said she had read that to save the peach stone the trouble of turning over, it must be put into the ground with the stem end down and the pointed end up. She said that after it had been in the ground for a certain time the stone opened, like a pocket-book, and the kernel came out in a twist at first, and then spread itself out into tiny leaves.

None of the rest of us had read that, but we all believed it, only Caro insisted that we were at a funeral, and pretended to cry, just to tease us. Caro said it would never do to give the poor stone cause to turn in its grave! And so it· was planted with the stem end downward.

We built a pen of pine sticks around it, and said that if it ever grew it was to be called Em's tree.

Just after the planting, Judge, who had been looking more solemn than usual, went up to Em and said, "Hold fast what I give you!" and when Em shut her eyes and put out her hand to "hold fast," Judge slipped something into her hand and ran off as fast as his legs could carry him.

Em "held fast" a second, then she opened her hand and looked — and there was such a tiny basket.

It was a little larger than her thumb-nail. It was brown all over. The whole of the basket, even the handle, was in one piece. There was not a seam or a put-together part in it; it was all one.

Judge had cut this wee basket from his peach stone. The stem end of the stone made the bottom of the basket, and the pointed end was the handle. A three-cornered section had been cut out evenly from each side of the stone, leaving a line to the point on either side for the handle of the basket. Then the kernel had been cut and lifted out, and the hollow where it had been made a tiny place for the inside of the basket.

So the event of the giving of the peaches had been made memorable in two ways, for the peach stone that Doc planted grew and bore splendid peaches for many years, and it was always called Em's tree; and the basket that Judge cut from the peach stone was a lasting pleasure to many little girls, for many little boys took it for a pattern by which to cut other baskets as pretty and as tiny.

It takes a sharp knife, though, and much care and patient work to make a peach-stone basket.

CHAPTER V

GOOSE QUILLS

"I WONDER why it is that we always have goose on Michaelmas Day," said Judge.

He was lying on his back, half way down one of the rose terraces in our Grandmother's garden, his hands were clasped behind his head, and he was looking up at the blue, blue sky of September.

"Aunts said we had goose to bring good luck," said Doc.

"Grandma said 'Nonsense,'" said Amy.

"Aunty Jean said we had goose on Michaelmas to put money in the purse all the year round," said Elise, the hopeful, who always found a good reason to believe all good things possible.

"Grandma said 'Nonsense,'" again reminded Doc.

"Grandma knows," said Caro, finally.

"Of course she does," said Amy.

"Then why is it?" persisted Judge.

Then the next oldest grandchild, the one who was near-sighted and always squinting over books, said, "One reason may be —"

"Don't say anything about Rome," said Judge, sitting up straight on the terrace. Judge loved a story, and though he was too lazy to read books to find out the stories for himself, he was always ready to hear them told; but then they always had to be new. For he said when you had heard one you could think it over and change and arrange it to suit yourself. So he said: "Please don't say anything about a goose saving Rome."

"No," said the oldest grandchild; "for we finished Rome last year!"

The next oldest grandchild squinted up her eyes a little more and said: "I wasn't going to say anything about Rome. I was going to say that I have heard that it was on

Michaelmas Day that Queen Elizabeth happened to be eating a goose when news was brought to her of the defeat of the Spanish Armada, — and in her joy at the news she said: 'Let every good Englishman ever after eat a goose on Michaelmas Day!'"

All the grandchildren looked very solemn as they thought over that.

"But how was every good Englishman to get a goose?" asked Judge.

Judge always loved to pick over his stories when he got them.

"Raise them," said Doc.

"The Spanish Armada seems very far off from us," said Elise; "and besides, we are not good Englishmen. I would rather believe what Aunts said about the good luck and the money in the purse all the year round."

"But Grandmother said 'Nonsense!'" said the oldest grandchild.

"And Grandma knows," they all repeated.

"It seems a pity to stop believing things,"

said Elise; "because Aunts were saying to-day
that when they were little girls they believed
that about money in the purse all the year
round, and that on the first Michaelmas Day
when they had heard about the money Grandpa
laughed about it, but he gave them all around
(Aunts were very little then) a silver picayune.
And Aunts said that they had those picayunes
yet — and that seems like a sign!"

"But Grandma said 'Nonsense!'" insisted
Amy.

"When Aunts were so little, Grandma was
not a Grandma," said Judge.

Now that came of Judge's thinking so much!
that came of his lying on his back and thinking so much, for only much, much thinking
could have brought up a thought like that!

"That seems strange," said the oldest
grandchild, in almost a whisper.

Then we all sat in a row and thought, for it
seemed to us, all ten grandchildren here on the
rose terraces, that we were somehow respon-

sible for Grandma's being a Grandma, — and
we felt that the responsibility was great!
Because now, being a grandmother, our Grandmother knew all things — things that we were
sure only grandmothers could know; and she
knew above all, and knew so positively, when
to say "Nonsense!"

While we thought hard over all these strange
matters, there came toward us Grandmother's
own little black maid, Dilsey.

As soon as she reached us, Dilsey said: "Ole
Miss say for all de grandchildren please to
come to her room."

"What do you suppose she wants?" asked
the oldest grandchild.

"What does Grandma want us for, Dilsey?"
asked the youngest grandchild of all.

Dilsey only kept rolling her hands and arms
in her blue-checked apron, as she always did,
and said nothing, but she laughed as she
skipped along a little behind the row of grandchildren as they walked to the house.

"It isn't fair to ask Dilsey if Grandma didn't tell her to tell us," said Doc. Of course we all knew that, except perhaps the youngest grandchild of all.

"We shall know soon enough," said Judge.

Judge never did mind waiting for anything. It seemed to give him more time for thinking and enjoying. But to be sure we did know soon enough and we enjoyed the gifts all the more for not having known before.

For as soon as we entered Grandmother's room we saw on her candle table (the table that tilted that way and this way, first for a fire-screen and then for a table) the most beautiful little chairs arranged in a row. The chairs were all alike, snow-white and delicately fairy-like in appearance. There were as many chairs as there were granddaughters.

That is the good of being a girl, — there are things that girls can have that nobody ever thinks of giving to boys.

But Grandmother never left out the boys,
either. On the corner of the same table were
goose-quill pens. There was a goose-quill
pen for each grandson. Grandmother had
cut them herself in the "good old-fashioned
way."

It was not until Grandmother had given
the boys their pens and had shown them how
to make more, that we who were girls realized
that our chairs were made of goose-quills, too!
Our chairs were the prettiest presents.

But the boys did not mind that, for they
felt very important with their pens, and with
knowing how to make others like them, for
they thought they were, as Grandmother had
said, "the young people who were helping to
keep an old art from being lost."

It was not long before the boys learned,
from looking carefully at our chairs, how to
make feather chairs also. They were made,
those chairs, of pins and of goose-quills
stripped of all of the feathers except just

enough to make the seat of the fine, snow-white chair.

So afterwards the grandchildren who were boys often made goose-feather chairs for the grandchildren who were girls; and we always called them Michaelmas chairs.

CHAPTER VI

CLOVER WREATHS

WE did not often go to the Far Pasture, those of us of the ten grandchildren who were little girls. That was our strange land. We knew that the boys found material there for the wonderful cane whistles, the hickory whistles, and the sweet-sounding cane flutes that they sometimes brought us. And wonder of wonders! sometimes the boys found there a nest of partridge eggs. We who were little girls did not go often enough even to remember how things looked, except that everything in the Far Pasture was wide and large.

The Near Pasture was our own, or we thought it was! There the gentlest old cows grazed, scarcely lifting their heads to look at us as we gathered clover blossoms from under their very noses. There were so many kinds of clover: there was the sharp, pointed, red bloom of the clover; there was the round, white bloom like a lady's powder puff; there was the loose purple blossom; there was the lowly little yellow clover; there was the tall, swinging white mellilotus, as tall as the tallest of us, and so sweet that its leaves, as we ran through them, sent a perfume over all the earth, — at least we thought it went over all the earth.

We made long chains and wreaths of clover. We made them of one color or of all colors. This was the way we made them: we gathered a heap of the blossoms with the slim, soft stems attached. The slim, green stem of one was tied close to the head of another blossom in a tight little knot of its own, each little stem tied close to the next little head, until a long wreath was made. Then we called out:

"Who shall be the Queen?" Then we answered: "The one that first finds the four leaf clover shall be the Queen."

Then we fell to hunting the field over for the lucky leaves. When one little girl found a four leaf clover, we all ran to the one with the lucky leaf and crowned her Queen of the Clover Band. We took the four leaf clover that she had found and set it like a carved emerald in front of the clover blossom wreath that we placed on her head. Then for all the rest of that afternoon we obeyed our Queen.

If she said: "Caro, sing a song!" then Caro had to sing her very best. If she said: "Doc, dance a highland fling!" then Doc danced a little highland fling as best he could. If the Queen of the Clover Band said: "Tell the best story you can," then we had a good story about knights and ladies or about fairies. To be sure there were some afternoons when two little girls found the lucky leaves at the same time! Then we had two Queens. Two Queens of the Clover Band! Dear me, that kept us busy. We were all busy bees in the clover then. You do not know how busy unless you have had to obey two Queens yourself, and to obey both at the same time! It was then dance and sing and jump and run all in a whirl, just as fast as the two Queens with the four leaf clover on their brows could think! Clover play was great fun, for we could have Queens all May Month as well as May Day.

But to be sure there was one afternoon when none of us ten grandchildren found a four leaf clover, and yet that was the most memorable afternoon of all. As we were playing in the Near Pasture, who should come walking there but Aunts and the Captain and the Lieutenant. No sooner had they sat upon a grassy knoll, Aunts with their tiny slippers tucked so neatly under their ruffled skirts, than we all came, all ten of us, and sat

in a semicircle about them. We felt that
somehow we must play host and hostess in
our favorite playground, that we must enter-
tain our appreciated company. Appreciated,
but, looking back, it hardly seemed appreciative company! For after we had explained to
the Captain how we made the finder of the four
leaf clover our Queen, he pointed to some far
distant places, urging us to seek there the lucky
leaf. Readily we all scampered to the distant
spots, where long and faithful search failed to
reward us, Aunts laughing all the time at our
fruitless endeavors. Once, when we returned
from our farthest search, Youngest Aunt said
to the Captain, — Amy heard her say it and
reported to the rest, — "Yes, if one lucky leaf
is found, I promise, I promise to say 'Yes.'"

Then to be sure the Captain searched as
hard and as far afield as we, and as fruitlessly.
Long since Other Aunt and the Lieutenant
had left the knoll to walk up and down the
path beside the brook. ·

After a particularly long search on the part of the Captain he returned to the knoll where Youngest Aunt sat laughing softly. The Captain was very warm, for his gray, brass-buttoned coat was heavy and he was fanning himself with his military cap. He threw himself on the knoll beside Youngest Aunt, shaking his head sadly. We all, all ten of us, came straggling after

THE CAPTAIN

and seated ourselves in a semicircle about the knoll.

"No leaf?" asked Aunt.

"No leaf at all," said the Captain, sadly.

Then Youngest Aunt lifted her hand from

the grass where it had lain during all the Captain's many warm searches, which he called his "fruitless forages" and "forced marches," and there — just under Aunt's hand — was a four leaf clover.

It seemed to us, all ten of us, that Aunt might have told the Captain and so saved him from all those forced marches, but when we said so Aunt only laughed the more. And the Captain laughed when he saw it. "Your promise," said the Captain. "The four leaf clover is found, and at last — "

"It was there all the time for you, —" said Youngest Aunt, softly, and when their fingers met in plucking it Aunt's cheeks were red as the reddest of the clover blossoms.

"She must be the Queen of the Royal Leaf," cried Caro.

"Queen of my heart," we thought we heard the Captain say, but we could not be sure, for Aunt cried so suddenly: "The children! remember the children!"

Just then Other Aunt and the Lieutenant came slowly sauntering up from the brook path, and — strange indeed ran the luck that afternoon — Aunt was twirling two four leaf clovers in her fingers.

When Youngest Aunt saw this, she cried "Oh !"

And Other Aunt, at something she saw, or thought she saw, cried "Oh, Oh !" Then they all laughed happily, and it seemed to us a little foolishly, for, after all, had not many four leaf clovers been found there before?

Judge said, — I think he thought something serious lay beneath all the happy laughter, — Judge said: "It is rich ground that bears so many four leaf clovers."

"Yes," said Doc, who always spoke very true and practical words; "Yes, this is a promising field."

At that the Captain laughed more than ever and those four grown people went straight to our Grandmother upon their return to the house and told her that they had been to the Promising Field.

After that the Near Pasture was always called the Promising Field. Why, we, the ten grandchildren, were to know only later, much later. But that afternoon, when none of us, that is, none of us ten grandchildren, had found a four leaf clover, was the afternoon that gave us most matter for talk together.

CHAPTER VII

HALLOWE'EN WITCHES

THE parlor at Grandmother's house was thirty feet long. It seemed to us grandchildren a great room. There were folding doors between it and the small back parlor. We ten grandchildren could not imagine a longer space enclosed by walls than that back and front parlor when the folding doors were opened. One day in autumn both rooms were decorated in red and gold leaves, and we were told that that evening we might try our fortunes. We did not understand exactly what that meant, but we thought it best to talk it over among ourselves before we asked. We went, all ten of us, to the round bed about which the green box bushes grew. There we dropped, each of us, into the side of a round, green box bush. The box bush stood stiff, and

held each child like a green chair with green back
and arms all in one. Whenever we were found
sitting in a semicircle in the box bushes we
were told to get up at once or we would ruin
the box bushes by sitting in them. We always got up obediently, but there was always a
"next time" when we went back to the box
bushes. So we sat there in a semicircle in
the sun, and wondered what "trying fortunes"
could be.

Judge said that a fortune was money; not
the blue paper we thought all the world had
now, which we heard the negroes call "Jeff
Davis money," but yellow gold money, a
great deal of it, which was found in old rusty
pots or in caves, or rolled out of sail cloth
bags in rich floods and heaps. That sounded
pleasant and probable to us.

Doc said that he had heard much talk among
grown people of the fortunes of war. Young
as we were, we, too, knew something of the
fortunes of war, most of which seemed to us ill

fortunes, and we were not pleased with that idea, so we turned about uneasily in our box bush chairs.

Then the next oldest grandchild came to our rescue, as she often did, for much reading out of books is, after all, good for something. She said she had often read that Fortune was a fairy prince. Now we liked that! But we wondered what we would do if fairy princes came. We had now in the house a Lieutenant and a Captain, and we hardly knew what we ought to do with them. If it had not been for Aunts, the responsibility would have been too great for us. We now began to wonder with one accord what they were doing — the Captain and the Lieutenant. Our sense of duty rose within us, and we determined, the six of us who were girls, to go to see if they were being properly entertained. The boys refused to obey this fancied call of duty, and instead they went to the Far Pasture to play.

In what a plight we found the Captain and

the Lieutenant! The Captain and one Aunt were at one end of the long parlor. He was holding on his hands a hank of home-grown, home-spun, home-dyed wool, while Aunt wrapped the thread off his hands into a ball.

At the other end of the back parlor the Other Aunt and the Lieutenant were sitting. He was doing absolutely nothing — only watching her as she made tatting.

We felt that we had not come to the rescue a moment too soon. We knew how lonely we should have felt in such a plight. On the instant we divided our forces evenly and went to the rescue of both parties, besieged, we felt sure, with the terror of loneliness. Three of us went to where the Youngest Aunt and the Captain were winding wool, and we seated ourselves in a row on the ottoman in front of them.

The other three of us dragged three straight-backed parlor chairs in front of Aunt and the Lieutenant. They need not be lonely now!

Then the four of them, who had seemed so silent but a moment before, all at once began to talk. They told us of the fortunes to be told on Hallowe'en night. They were going to hang up a cross beam with a candle at one end and an apple at the other. As the swinging beam turned we were to try to bite the apple as a sign for good luck, or a fairy prince, or something to come. We were to dive our heads into a tub of water in which apples were floating, and to try to bite those floating apples. Or we could burn nuts on the hearth, or wind a strand of yarn from a ball of blue wool, and, throwing one end out of a window, call, "Who holds?" The fairy prince might be the one "who held."

The youngest granddaughter cried out in eager interest: "Just as the Captain holds the yarn now!"

And the eldest grandchild cried: "Of course, they are rehearsing."

For we knew much of rehearsing. We had often acted charades ourselves.

The Lieutenant said "Yes," and laughed very much, but the Captain did not laugh at all. Then Elise said that in books every fairy prince seemed to be in love. She hoped one would come that night, for she had always wished to see some one in love.

THE LIEUTENANT

"But," suggested the Lieutenant, "perhaps if you saw some one in love you might not know it."

"But suppose he should tell me that he was," argued Elise.

"That is surely what he would wish to do," said the Lieutenant.

"Oh," cried Elise, — for what better permis-

sion could she have had to ask a question,—
"perhaps you are in love?"

"Fie, Elise," cried Aunt.

But the brave Lieutenant did not falter, although the Captain was laughing now. "Yes,"
he said, "I am in love."

"But," said Elise, with a little touch of
disappointment, "you do not look any different
from the way you looked when I first saw you."

"Maybe, Elise, he has been in love since
the first day you saw him," suggested the
first grandchild.

The Lieutenant bowed very low to Elise,
and said: "How could it be otherwise? I
have been in love since the first moment I
saw you!"

The Lieutenant's eyes twinkled queerly, but
Elise never thought of the possibility of any
one's laughing at her, she was always so much
in earnest herself, so she sat undisturbed in
the straight-backed parlor chair and smiled
sweetly.

"Yes," said the Lieutenant very softly, "I think a certain little lady has as much sunshine in her heart as on her hair, as has some one else I know, and that, perhaps, is the reason why I fell in love."

ELISE

But we thought no more of fairy princes or of fortunes, because just then the boys came running in. They came from the Far Pasture where they had been playing, and they brought the funniest little midgets with them !

They had each made a little imp of a creature out of dry brown cockle-burrs. The head was a cockle-burr with bead eyes. Each

imp wore a red sumach leaf, pinned into a
dunce cap. Two cockle-burrs made each arm,
another made a hand, two cockle-burrs made
each leg, and one made each foot. They wore
coats of two sweet gum leaves pinned together,
one leaf red and one yellow. The points of the
leaves fell about them in an odd way.

The Lieutenant got up and took all the
midgets from the boys and put them among
the gold and yellow boughs that decorated the
parlor, so that they might, he said, look on at
the trying of fortunes that evening. Aunts
called the little imps Hallowe'en witches.
The boys offered to show us how to make more
of them, and we all ran to the edge of the Far
Pasture to gather cockle-burrs.

We went with an easy conscience, because
we thought we had done well toward enter-
taining company.

What Aunts and Company thought we did
not know.

CHAPTER VIII

TED'S THANKSGIVING

TED felt that he had never looked forward to a day with so many hopes. It was to be a Thanksgiving Day. That was a new sort of a day to Ted, new indeed to all of us; a day of thanks appointed by some high, if rather local dignitary, a forerunner of a Thanksgiving Day that was many years later to become a national institution appointed by presidents of a Union to which we were now outsiders. But we did not foresee that, for we were now out of the Union, and we believed that we were to be forever a nation to ourselves! No one had more plans for that especial new Thanksgiving Day than Ted.

And now he knew that not one of his plans could be carried out on that day, because he lay ill of a slow fever that would keep coming back to visit him every morning at ten and every afternoon at five. Ted grew so tired of that unwelcome little fever visitor.

It seemed to him that one of the worst trials of his enforced imprisonment in his mother's room was that he could hear, through the open window of the room, the sounds of stirring and "making up" of all sorts of good things to eat, things unusually good for these War times. Ted was not just then at our Grandmother's house, but at his other Grandmother's house in a small town. We often wondered how Ted, small and gentle as he was, almost the smallest of us ten grandchildren, could bear up under the great responsibility and honor of having two Grandmothers.

The room that his mother had there was on the wing that reached toward the kitchen, for of course all the kitchens in those days were apart from the house proper, and were good-sized houses in themselves.

When Ted was at his other Grandmother's
he was the only child in the house, and he
learned many ways of amusing himself, so
perhaps it was not as hard for him to stay
alone in one room as it would have been for
one of us, who had never in all our lives, or at
least not in our remembrance, been the only
child in the house.

One of his amusements at this time was
to "look over" the spools of thread in his
mother's "two-storied work basket." The
spools were always in the top story of the basket, and small rolls of scraps of colored cloth
were in the bottom story of the basket. Ted's
mother sat at the window in her low wicker
chair and sewed and mended and darned a
great part of the day, for there was much of
such work to be done in those days, as well as
the heavier weaving and spinning necessary
in War-time.

It seemed to Ted, as he lay there and looked
at his mother sewing, that almost every sec-

ond, — no, maybe it was every minute, or
maybe every other minute, — old Aunt Zilphy,
the cook, came to the window, to say to
Mother: "Young Miss, I have stoned de
raisins," or "Young Miss, I have blanched de
almonds." Or to ask: "Young Miss, is you
ready to make de roses and de curley-my-
cues on de cakes? De icing is mos' done."
"Ah, me," sighed Ted, when he heard of all
those good things in the making; "if I could
only eat raisins and nuts, I would not mind
missing the rest."

You see, raisins and almonds were very rare,
for, like most other things, they had to run
the blockade. Only home-raised, plantation
things were plentiful with us then.

It happened, after all, that just the day before the day that was to be Thanksgiving Day
the good doctor said: "No fever."

Then Ted's mother said: "Dear Ted, it is
to be *our* Thanksgiving Day after all."

Ted said: "Then I can eat raisins and nuts."

But the doctor said: "My, my, my! How does he come to think that!"

And Ted's mother said: "Dear me, dear me! What shall we do?"

Ted, who really felt worse than when the fever was with him, thought he must cry when the doctor said: "Not a nut, Ted, not a nut."

Ted was going to retreat slowly, if retreat he must, contending every point, so he said: "Raisins, doctor?"

The good doctor, who must have seen that Ted was about to cry, said: "My, my, my!"

Ted's mother then said for him — Ted told us all this when he was well enough to come again to our Grandmother's :— "doctor, two? or three, — only —"

But Ted said: "Six."

Then the doctor, looking very hard at Ted, who was winking so as not to cry, said: "If there is no fever when I come back — six."

Ted was glad, but he sighed, too, for the

next minute he thought how few six raisins were for a boy as big as he, a boy big enough to have four pockets when he was up and dressed.

Four pockets! Ted wished that he were up. An Alabama sling shot in one pocket, pebbles to shoot in it in another pocket, a penny and a picayune and a clean handkerchief in the third pocket, for Ted's mother made him promise to keep one pocket always fresh for a clean handkerchief; and nobody, nobody, nobody knew what Ted did keep in that other pocket: nails and strings and bullets and melted lead and snail shells and pieces of India rubber, — and what not — !

However, six raisins were something to think about, and that was a comfort when you had to stay all day upon one cot in one room. So Ted thought a great deal about the six raisins.

"Mother," Ted said, "Mother, I don't think I can enjoy six raisins very much, do you?"

But Ted's mother told him not to scorn a

Ted was Propped up on the Pillows

75

small good in wishing for a greater and impossible one.

The next day the queer little fever kept away, and how thankful Ted's mother and his other Grandmother and everybody was! So Ted was happy because everybody else was, Ted was that way. Ted had said: "I will wait for my six raisins until it is nuts-and-raisins time at the table for everybody."

So when nuts and raisins came to the table, Ted's mother herself left the table to take Ted his six raisins.

Ted was propped up on pillows waiting for her, and for the six raisins. She had in her hand a tiny silver tray, and over the tray was a tiny linen doily, and a red rosebud lay on top of the doily. Ted tried to look as cheerful (so he told us) as his mother was looking, but just at that moment six raisins had never seemed so few!

He lifted the little doily, and looked under it, and then he cried out: "Oh, Mother!"

What do you think Ted saw?

Six tiny turtles in a row.

Their tiny backs were of a reddish brown, rough and corrugated as real turtle-backs are. Each turtle had a tiny white head with black eyes. Each turtle had four little white feet, just showing from under their rough shells. Each turtle had a little white tail, — they looked for all the world like real, sure enough, live turtles.

Weak as Ted was, he laughed and laughed, and it seemed to him (so he told us) that the tiny turtles laughed back at him out of their little black-ink-dot eyes.

Then Ted said: "Mother, what are they?"

Ted's mother said: "Six raisins."

"But," said Ted, "they are so splendid."

But he would not eat them after all. He just looked at them and turned their tiny heads (which were bits of blanched almond with ink-dot eyes) this way and that way to make them look in different directions; and by giving a touch to their almond legs he could make them look as if they were creeping, as turtles creep, or running as slowly as turtles run, or just resting.

When he had enjoyed them a long time, he asked his mother to put them away so that he could enjoy them to-morrow and other days, and he said to his mother: "Mother, I never thought anybody could enjoy six raisins so *very* much; did you?"

CHAPTER IX

A THANKSGIVING GENTLEMAN

CARO and Em sat at one end of the long arbor, the butter-bean arbor in Grandmother's garden. The arbor was a long green tunnel, cool and shady even at midday. It was a favorite play-place for the ten grandchildren; but to-day only Caro and Em were there. That day Grandmother had talked to the children about the harvest home festivals of long ago. She told us how, in the good old days, the slaves were allowed to hold high festival at the Quarters how they came to the Great House on those festive occasions, and, calling out the Master, lifted him on to the shoulders of four of the strongest slaves and carried him about the green in front of the House, with songs of thanksgiving. Now all the masters had gone to the War, but the crops had been good and the cribs and cotton houses were filled to overflowing, and Grandmother said that in spite of war and of deprivation of foreign goods, we ought at this season to have a spirit of thanksgiving. Judge went off, we felt sure, to meditate upon the matter. Doubtless we should, all ten of us, later profit by his thoughts; if we did not, Judge would make us feel that it was our own fault.

Em and Caro had gone to the bean arbor, and there they tried to get up a Thanksgiving spirit. It was very hard work for little girls who did not know how. They each rolled up a large pumpkin, from the newly gathered heap at the end of the arbor, and sat upon it. "Now," said Caro, "we are like two princesses seated upon ottomans of gold in a long palace hall of glittering malachite."

"Oh, Caro, you think of such strange things," said Em; "you ought to be thankful for that, for it saves so much reading just to be able to think up tales for yourself."

"Well," said Caro, "then I will be thankful, and, if you are thankful about it, too, why then, Em, we have, without any trouble, a spirit of thanksgiving."

"Oh, it can't be just that," said Em. "If Judge were here we might ask him —"

But the little boy coming down the garden walk was Doc and not Judge, and it was no use asking Doc about anything that you could not see with your eyes or touch with your hands. Doc cared only for practical things. Just as he reached the arbor his foot caught on something, and he stopped to loosen it. "It's an old devil's-claw," said he, holding up the thing that had caught his foot.

"I thought they were martynia," said Em.

"So many things have two and even three names," said Caro.

Em reached for the martynia, and said: "Oh, how funny it looks, like an old man with crooked feet." She set it up against one of

G

the poles of the arbor. "It's a Thanksgiving visitor come to see us."

"Where is its head?" asked Doc. Doc could not imagine things. Caro reached through the bean vines to where the gherkins grew, and pulled off a gherkin that was so old that it was turning yellow. She stuck it on the stem of the martynia, and said: "There is its head."

ONE OF THE TEN

"Now," said Em, "we will name him Mr. Gherkin Martynia."

"That is a fine name," said Caro; "now shut your eyes and I will dress him as he should be." Then Em and Doc shut their eyes, and when Caro called to them to open their eyes the Thanksgiving gentleman was dressed as he should be. He had two round spice eyes, a clove stuck in long-ways for a nose, a slice of red pepper for his mouth, and seeds of the pepper for his teeth. Half of a large red bell pepper made his cap, a cap like an Eastern fez. Another martynia put around the first made two claw-like arms, and some bean leaves hung like a cape about the queer gentleman. When Em and Doc saw the queer little gentleman, they laughed and laughed. Caro laughed too, but then she said: "He doesn't look funny to me any more."

"Why?" said Em.

"He looks so dry and old," said Caro.

"He misses being where he ought to be," said Doc.

"Why, where ought he to be?" said Em.

"In the pickle jar," said Caro.

"Oh, he is too old for the pickle jar," said Em.

"That's just what he is sorry about," said

Caro; "he thinks it is hard to be too old to carry out the purpose for which he was created."

"Dear me," sighed Em, looking dejectedly at the queer gentleman.

"But, Caro," said Doc; "anyhow he has with him the things he would have around him in the pickle jar, pepper, spice, and cloves."

"Oh, Doc, that is true," cried Em; "I'm so glad, I'm sure he may be thankful, too."

"Let's ask him," said Caro, "if he can now be thankful for small mercies —"

So the three children took hands and stood in front of Mr. Gherkin Martynia, whose queer red fez made him look like a real Grand Turk, and they said, bowing all together: "Mr. Gherkin Martynia, we have done all that we could for you. In spite of your being too old for the pickle jar, we have put the nice things and the spice things of the pickle jar about you. Are you happier?"

TWO OF THE TEN

Then the three lifted themselves from their
very deep bows and stood in silence before the
queer gentleman. "Perhaps — maybe — "
suggested Caro; "it might have been the
shadow of a leaf, but it seemed to me that
perhaps — maybe — he bowed his head."

"Oh," said Em.

"If he did," said Caro, "we might as well
believe that he is happier, and that he
has some sort of a thanksgiving spirit for
himself."

"Oh, I hope so !" said Em.

"Shall we take him and show him to the
others, Doc ?" asked Caro; "for there is our
children's table bell ringing now."

"No, let him alone," said Doc; "the sight
of really truly pickles might make him sad
again, and we don't want that."

"Indeed we don't," declared Em, upon
whose soul Mr. Gherkin Martynia dejection
had weighed heavily. So the three children
ran in to the children's table, and that night

a rain came up and washed Mr. Gherkin
Martynia off down the bean arbor path and
into the brook, away, away, and away, and
neither Caro, nor Doc, nor even Em, ever
thought of him any more.

CHAPTER X

THE CHRISTMAS STALK

EM sat under the wide fig-tree, thinking.

She had had a great many toys that morning, and they were real toys, no "pretend" about them. For all the best old toys in the family had been brought from their hiding-places and sent on to us, because we had had no real toys since War-time. The swans really followed the magnet round and round in the basin of water! The toy wagons really ran! But do you know, Em was already tired of them all! and yet she felt ashamed of being tired, even the least bit tired, of such wonderful things. So she sat under the wide fig-tree and thought.

Presently through the trees of the orchard she saw Caro coming. Caro was coming straight to the fig-tree, the wide one where

Em sat thinking. Caro, being older than Em, knew better than Em how tired one grows of even the prettiest toys.

Em watched her coming across the orchard.

Caro carried a dry, yellow corn-shuck in her hand.

She stood in front of Em where she sat under the wide fig-tree: "Em, I'm going to tell you a story with some maybe in it."

"Oh," said Em, "I'm so glad! And Caro, sometimes I think those with maybe's in them are better than those with the all-sures."

"Well, that is only sometimes," said Caro.

"Won't you sit down?" said Em, for she was a very polite little girl, — even to her sister.

"No," said Caro; "I'll stand up." And Caro stood up with her red curls almost touching the broad leaves of the fig-tree, for, though it was Christmas Day, no heavy frost had fallen in Alabama, and the fig leaves were still green.

"You know," began Caro, "the field hands do not knock down and burn the corn stalks until January, when they begin to get ready for next year's plowing."

"Yes, I know," said Em.

"Well, you know how the fodder is pulled in midsummer, and tied on to the stalk, and how the hands haul the fodder to the cribs and barns?"

"Yes, and isn't it fun to get in the crib loft, while the men are throwing up the bundles of fodder, and counting the hundreds, — isn't it fun to play in the bundles and let them fall all over us!"

"Yes, it is fun," said Caro. "Then, you know how the corn in the shuck is left on the stalk in the fields until it is quite dry."

"Yes," said Em; "and it is fun to ride from the fields on the wagons full of corn when Uncle Jake drives them in —"

"Yes, that is the most fun," said Caro; "and suppose, Em, that there should be one — just one — stalk left in the corner of the fence where the hands could not see it, under the dry blackberry bushes, and the sarsaparilla vines, you know, and suppose it should be left with ears still on it, and suppose that one stalk should be 'The Christmas stalk' —"

"Would the ears on it be different from any other ears of corn?" asked Em.

"They might be," said Caro.

"Oh," said Em; "Caro, is that one in your hand from the — 'Christmas stalk'?"

"It might be," said Caro.

"Is the ear on it red?" asked Em.

"Pshaw," said Caro; "there are red ears all the time, any time. I know Dicie has brought us a hundred red ears from the corn shuckings."

"Yes, I suppose she has," said Em.

"This is a young lady," said Caro.

"A young lady!" cried Em.

"Don't you see that it is a young lady?"

"We might pretend so," said Em, cheer-
fully; "and that ridgy stem you are holding
her by might be her head — but —"

"But what?"

"She wouldn't look much like one —"

"Well, whether she looks like one to you
or not, there is a young lady here." Caro
tapped the shuck so positively that Em was
deeply impressed, — but still the shuck did
not look like a young lady. Em thought it
best not to say anything more just yet.

"She has an Indian name," said Caro.

"Oh, like the Virginians!" said Em.

"Only those who are related to Pocahontas
have Indian names," corrected Caro.

"I thought they were all related to Pocahontas, so many have told me they were kin
to her," said Em.

"All who are related tell you so," said
Caro; "and those who are not don't say anything about it."

"Oh!" said Em.

"Well, this young lady's name is 'Miss Maize'!"

"That is a very pretty name," said Em.

"That is what the Indians called her," said Caro; "and now if you want to, you may be the one to take her out of the shuck —"

And Caro turned the shuck around.

"Oh," cried Em. She had thought of fairies and of things like that all her life, — and had always expected to see a fairy beneath every mushroom under which she peeped, — but this black-eyed young lady with her real auburn fluffy hair, and her red mouth, all fully dressed in golden stuff, was something more than she had ever expected to see. Caro held out the shuck to her, but she could not touch it. It was too wonderful. The young lady was lying close to the shuck, too, just as an ear of corn lies.

"You won't take her out?" said Caro.

"Caro, I don't think I *can*," said Em, pleasurable awe in her tones.

"Well, here she is," said Caro. And she gently opened the shuck,, and lifted out the young lady, and stood her on the ground under the wide fig-tree.

Whether the young lady's dress was of stiff cloth of gold, or of richest silk, Em did not quite know yet — but the dress was stiff and crisp enough to stand alone.

"And the bonnet —" gasped Em, when she had breath enough to speak.

"Yes, she is a Quakeress," said Caro.

"Oh !" said Em, for she thought that this young lady was wonderful enough to be related to Pocahontas and to be a Quakeress, too.

"But I believe it is the Shakers, and maybe not the Quakers, that wear such bonnets," said Caro, thoughtfully.

"Well, it doesn't make any difference which," said Em; "for either way she is beautiful."

"And she grew on the Christmas stalk," said Caro.

"I believe it," said Em.

"Now, I'll tell you really how it was that she grew," said Caro; "she is made of corn pith."

"Oh," said Em.

"Yes, and her stiff golden dress is the clean inside of a shuck from the ear. And when you pull off the shuck from the stem it fits around so — as if it were made to go around a waist, and so two pieces of shuck make a skirt."

"Oh, I see," said Em.

"Then two more cut shorter make an over-skirt," said Caro; "and the other end of the shuck curves in so as to fit the neck, and there is her cape-waist."

"Oh, yes," said Em.

"Her arms are two little pieces of outside cornstalk, — and her sleeves are, of course, cut out of the scraps of cloth-of-gold left from cutting her skirts and waist."

"She is beautiful," said Em.

"Her eyes are two black-headed pins. I took a dip out of mother's black ink for her lashes and brows, and a dip out of her red ink for her mouth; and her bonnet—"

"Oh, her bonnet!" said Em.

"Well, the end of a small shuck fitted exactly for that! I only had to put on a small flap behind, and the flowers were easily cut out of the shuck."

"After all," said Em, with a sigh of great delight, "Miss Maize did somehow grow on the Christmas stalk."

"Yes, she did," said Caro.

"Caro," said Em, very thoughtfully, "I like her better than I do all the real toys. I suppose it is because we have had pretend toys so long that we like that kind best."

"Maybe so," said Caro. "Or maybe they are best for children—for War-time children, anyhow."

CHAPTER XI

A QUEER HATCHING

WE always felt serious on Easter Eve, we grandchildren. We practised our Easter carols on Easter Eve. This practising was done in an arbor in the far woodland, — an arbor that our Aunts called Sans Souci. No one from the house could hear our singing from the arbor, so on Easter morning our carols were a surprise to our mothers and our Grandmother, when we sang them outside of their bedroom windows. Only our two younger aunts knew of the carols. They had to know, because they taught them to us. It was strange that the other grown-up people were so delightfully surprised every time, for we did the same way every year; yet surprised they always were on Easter Morning. We, of course, were glad that we had such a surprise for them!

A Queer Hatching

As has been said, we always felt serious on Easter Eve. This evening we felt more serious than usual. Every Easter before this there had always been an egg hunt. It came just after the singing of the carols outside the windows. When we had so delightfully surprised the grown people, we were always equally surprised ourselves by finding, in all sorts of unexpected places, the eggs that the Easter Hen had laid. Sometimes we found them, beautiful eggs of all colors, hidden in the box bushes that grew around the circular bed, in the midst of which stood the sun-dial. Sometimes we found the eggs, half hidden in moss and fern, by the side of the brook that ran through the back of Grandmother's garden. Sometimes even, the boys (for four of us grandchildren were boys and six were girls) climbed up into a tree and found big, bright-colored eggs in the last years' nests left by the mocking-birds. So, no matter how serious we had felt on every other Easter Evening before this, we could cheer ourselves by thinking of the egg hunt on the morrow. But on this Easter Eve Grandmother had said: "No, there will be no Easter eggs this year. These children are too old for Easter eggs."

Well, Grandmother always spoke the truth. Whatever Grandmother said, that thing would surely happen, or had already happened. Well, well! Something had happened to us, and until that minute we had not known it! We had grown too old for Easter eggs!

We sat in a row on the top step of the long, broad flight of steps that led from the flower garden to the broad piazza, on which the French windows of the parlor opened. We sat in a row looking at the budding lilies in the garden beyond, and we felt very serious indeed.

Judge spoke first: "It is very strange," he said, "that we all grew too old at once."

"How do you mean?" asked Doc, who did not think as much or as fast as Judge did.

"Well, you see," said Judge; "you are nearly fourteen, and Willy-boy is only four."

"Oh, I see," said Doc; "and all at once we were both too old!"

"It is that way," said Amy; "it is obliged to be that way with Easter eggs, because Grandmother has said so."

"Of course," said Judge; "it is that way. Only it is strange."

"It seems strange to us," said Em; "because it has never happened to us before."

"It is that way with things when they are new," said Caro. "Now Mother says that war seems strange to her, with everybody, that is all the men-people, doing nothing, nothing at all but having battles. But that doesn't seem strange to me. What else could the men-people be doing? I never heard of men-people doing anything but marching, holding forts, having furloughs, and fighting battles. Mother says that war doesn't seem strange to us because we can't remember very

far back, and have known only war, but
Mother says she has known peace."

"Well," said Doc, "the only way to do is
just to get used to things as they are."

Then Ted, who was little and round and who
tried to be happy about everything, said:
"Let's play 'I spy' in the yard until Grandma
sends Dilsey to ring our go-to-bed-bell."

So we ran into the yard to hide, all but Doc.
He was to be first counter. He sat on the
corner of the bottom step (that was to be the
base), and shut his eyes. He had to count a
hundred before he could open his eyes and
begin to seek us in our hiding-places. We
told him to count a hundred just straight
along and aloud, by ones, — not by tens, nor
by fives, nor by the very fast way: "Ten!
ten! double ten! forty-five and fifteen!"

So we played "I spy" until our go-to-bed-
bell rang, and the next morning we were up
bright and early to sing our carols outside the
windows. We sang at Grandmother's win-

dow last. We sang our best and brightest carol there. No sooner had we finished singing than Dilsey, Grandmother's own black maid, who had been peeping at us from between the curtains of Grandmother's windows, came to the door of Grandmother's room and flung it wide open, and said: —

"Little Ladies and Gen'lemen! Ole Miss say: 'Come in!'"

We were amazed. Grandmother's door was open; it was always open; few, if indeed any of us ten grandchildren, had ever seen that door shut. But was it possible that Grandmother was ready to give us our morning audience at this early hour? We looked at one another all down the row of the ten of us.

Dilsey laughed and said again: "Ole Miss say y'all come in. I 'spec' the Easter hen has hatched."

We went in.

We *were* surprised at what we saw. There

on Grandmother's candle-table were ten of the
queerest birds we had ever seen !

There was a hollow tree-trunk, built of bark,
and just in front of that hollow tree, were
seated two wee owls. Their gray wings were
spread out from their sides, and they looked
with wise eyes toward each other. Next to
the hollow tree there was a small piece of rail
fence, built of bits of kindling wood, and on the
top rail of the fence sat two black buzzards !
buzzards with shoulders humped up, just as
real buzzards hump up their shoulders ! On
the top of the table stood a turkey gobbler with
outspread wings and tail, and opposite to him
was a peacock, in all the glittering glory of
his fan-shaped tail and wide wings. There
was also a deep saucer with moss around it,
and a snow-white swan floated on the water
in the saucer. Over on one side of the table
was a white gander, and beside him an
old gray goose. From a thread suspended
over the table an eagle was poised on open

wings hanging over all the rest of the curi-
ous birds.

It was indeed a queer hatching.

We stood, all ten of us, around the table, and
looked with wondering eyes at the strange
birds.

"Each take one," said Grandmother. "See
how they are made."

"Made!" we cried. Each one of us ten
grandchildren cried: "Made!"

"Take them and run away," said Grandmother.

And we did.

And after all those birds were Easter eggs!
The eggs were dyed, or painted, in different
colors. Those that were made into buzzards
were dyed black. Those that were made into
owls were gray. The turkey cock was brown,
the peacock, blue, and so on through the list
of birds. Each egg was colored to match the
bird it was to represent. The wings, the
tails, the heads, and the necks were made of

different colored tissue papers, folded and twisted into the proper shapes. The birds all had bead eyes sewed in. The legs and feet of the birds were made of matches wound with yellow silk thread. These were glued to the eggs with sealing wax, as were the wings, tails, and heads of folded tissue paper.

When we had all admired our birds, Doc said: "I am glad, after all, that we are too old for easter egg hunts."

Ted said: "I am glad we all grew too old just at one time, all ten of us together."

CHAPTER XII

A DOWNY CHICK

IT was the very next Easter after we had suddenly, all ten of us at once, grown too old for hunting colored Easter eggs, that Ted's mother brought him back to our Grandmother's so that we could all be together at Easter. Ted had another Grandmother; the wonder of that never ceased for us, — two Grandmothers! That Grandmother lived in a town, and when Ted was not living with us and our Grandmother, he was living there in town with his Other Grandmother.

All Easter morning we had listened for the carriage that was to bring Ted and his mother, and when we heard the pleasant grating sound, a quarter of a mile away, as the wheels crunched down the gravel hill, we all scampered to the gate to meet Ted and his mother.

108

THE OTHER GRANDMOTHER'S HOME

109

Aunts ran to the gate, too, and even our mothers. Because that was the way that we did when any one came to see us: we ran to the gate to meet them. All but Grandmother: she sat in her chair in the corner by the fire, with her feet on the footstool and the round cushion at her back, and all the people who came, whoever they were, went first to Grandmother's room and said "how do you do," to her. Sometimes it was Bishops who came, sometimes Generals, sometimes only the Captain and the Lieutenant, sometimes kinsfolk, as it was to-day; but whoever it was, they always went first to Grandmother's room to speak to her.

While the servants were taking the bags and portmanteaus and the bonnet-box from the rack and boot of the carriage, Ted whispered to us that he had something to show us. He said that it was a gift to him, but that all of us could have it partly for ours, too.

"All of us can have it partly for ours?" asked Willy-boy.

And Ted said: "Yes, all of us."

So we were naturally anxious to see what the gift might be. We followed Ted's mother to Grandmother's room, and even before Aunts could unfasten and take off her bonnet and veil Ted was asking her for the white box, the small white box, his box. He stood by her chair and kept whispering in her ear and bumping his head against Aunts' elbows as they were trying to take off the bonnet and veil.

Then Ted's mother said: "Go, child! Go and bring me the carpet-bag. Let me see — — the flowered one!"

When she had opened the carpet-bag she gave into Ted's hand a small white box, and said: "Now, child!"

Doc, who always liked things done decently and in order, began to whisper to us: "The arbor, — let's go to the Honeysuckle Arbor."

Amy, who always helped Doc with his ordering of things, began to nudge us with her elbows as we stood all in a bunch, and to say: "Yes, the arbor."

We went, all of us, to the arbor, and stood about Ted, who had seated himself on the

round seat in the middle of the arbor. Ted held the box, and said: "Yesterday I went to see somebody I am very fond of, and Mother is fond of her too, and I told her how last Easter we had all grown too old to hunt Easter eggs, and how, after we had sung our carols, we had been asked to come into Grandmother's room to find there what Aunts called a queer hatching. The Somebody was very much interested in that idea. She said what I told her reminded her of something, and that she would send it to me early on Easter morning before we started for our Easter dinner here, and she did."

Ted began to untie the string about the box. Ted looked at us very solemnly, a way he often had, and said: "Mother says the Somebody who gave me this is a very lovely person, and she is — she is — a Maiden Lady."

Now that was something none of us had heard of before — a Maiden Lady. But it sounded very pleasant. The next oldest grandchild gave a gasp, and we knew that meant that she had suddenly thought of something that she had read in the books over which she was always poring. We looked at her and waited for her to speak. "It sounds like King Arthur's Table," she said; "the

Maidens have their hair flowing, with ribbons bound across their brows, though they are quite grown, and in picture books they are often sitting on deep window-seats with their hands clasped low on their knees; they often sit sideways and look out of the windows."

We grandchildren who were girls liked that. If we had been alone, we would have practised sitting that way with with our hands clasped low.

"But the lady part?" suggested Judge. Judge could never be satisfied to take a story just as it was.

"Ladies are oftenest, — in books —" said the Next Oldest Grandchild, "standing on the castle-turrets gazing out, or they are at the castle-gates giving bread to the clamoring poor."

Ted seemed a little puzzled at all this: "I think," he said (he had untied the string now), "I think it means that she has never married. I think Mother said that. But I *have* seen her at the gate giving hot ginger cakes that her old cook, Aunt Liz, had baked, to our soldier boys when they were marching through."

Ted had told us before of the soldier boys marching through. That is the good of living part of the time in a town. In the town there are streets for the soldiers to march through. We were all very quiet for a little while; for Ted had told us that though our soldier boys were all laughing and waving and cheering, they were ragged, and very thin. Everybody in any house in town who had any clothes or blankets or quilts, or anything ready to eat, had brought it out and given it to the soldier boys. Ted told us that he had given one of the soldiers his last Christmas red muffler, that Grandmother had knit for him with her own hands. He told us, as his mother had told him, that it was not often right to give away gifts, but that it was right to give them to the soldiers of our country.

We thought of all that, and it seemed to us very much in keeping with what the books had said that the Maiden Lady should stand at her gate and give hot ginger cakes to the soldiers.

"And she sent you the box early this morning?" asked Judge.

"Yes, very early," said Ted. "The gift is in the box." He opened the box.

All of us who were girls cried "Oh!"

Ted deftly lifted out a downy chick. You would have thought that it was real. That downy chick stood up on a little block of wood, covered with green velvet. With two black bead eyes the chick seemed to be looking down into a half egg-shell glued beside his yellow feet. His feet were made of match sticks wound with yellow silk thread. His body was a tiny round ball of cream zephyr wool. The chick was soft and beautiful.

We all ran to Grandmother's room to show the downy chick to our mothers and to our

A Downy Chick

117

aunts. Aunts said: "Do see! We, too, could make a Downy Chick."

Then Amy remembered that Ted had said that the Lovely Person who had made the downy chick had never married, and so she cried: "Oh, Aunts, can you? Then perhaps you will be Maiden Ladies! A Maiden Lady gave this to Ted —"

But Aunts cried: "Impertinent children!"

It seemed to us so beautiful an idea which Amy voiced that we all cried in a breath: "Oh! Yes — maybe — !"

Our mothers also cried: "Naughty children!"

Aunts blushed very red. We did not know why, unless it was with surprise at seeing through the open door the Captain and the Lieutenant dismounting from their horses at the hitching rack at the front gate. We were surprised, for we had not known, none of us ten grandchildren, that the Captain and the Lieutenant were coming to have Easter dinner with us.

CHAPTER XIII

LIGHTED CANDLES

THE four magnolia-trees were very tall and very wide and very thick. The trunks of those magnolia-trees were smooth and velvety and black. They were very thick magnolia-trees; all the year full of leaves, all the year shedding leaves, — so thick that when we looked up through them we could scarcely see a twinkle of blue sky, only green leaves and brown lining to the leaves, a lining soft and fine as brown velvet. Under those four wide magnolia-trees there was always a cool, great black shade, no matter how brightly the sun shone elsewhere. Under those four magnolia-trees we lit our candles.

On summer afternoons when the great round clock that hung in the hall struck, "One! Two! Three! Four!" we sprang up from whatever play we were at and said: "Time to light the candles."

Another child would cry: "Four o'clock."

Another would ask: "Are they opened yet?"

Judge would answer: "Just opening."

And Doc would say: "Let us go for sticks while they are opening."

Elise would cry: "Candlesticks!"

That seemed so funny that we all would laugh. The candlesticks that we gathered were long, slim peach switches. We stripped the bark off until they were as white as could be, and as we stripped them, we talked of all the lighted candles that we had seen. Some of us had seen lighted candles in the old Cathedral in Mobile; some of us had seen lighted candles on brides' tables, and some of us had seen lighted candles on Christmas trees, and all of us had had birthday candles of our own. When the sticks were stripped and white, we all ran to the flower garden, and some one cried: "They are open. They are wide open!"

Then one grandchild cried: "Mine shall be white!" Another said: "Mine shall be red!" Another, "Mine shall be yellow, very pale yellow!" "Mine, orange!" "Mine, rose-pink."

And we could make our candles of all those colors, just as we said. When we reached the flower yard, we cried all at once: "Oh, how sweet!" The whole yard was sweet — for They were all wide open, and They were — Four-o'clocks. We could gather as many as we pleased of these flowers; but, though we could gather as many as we chose, we were careful how we gathered the blossoms. We lifted only the round flower from the green socket upon which it grew, leaving on the stem buds for another day's blooming and the seed for another year's growing. So, lifting out the full round blossoms, we filled our hats, our aprons, our straw nunbonnets all full of them, each one gathering his or her chosen color. Then with our heaps of flowers we went to the cool shade of the magnolia-trees and there began to light our candles. It took us a long time to light the candles, for this was the way we lit them. We broke off carefully just enough of the tube of the four-o'clock to allow the blossom to slip over the slim candlestick, then we slipped the flower on the slim stick, then above it another flower, then another and another, until the whole stick was filled with flowers from top to bottom. When one candlestick was full of flowers the child who had filled it cried: "My candle is lighted." Another cried: "So is mine!" "And mine!" "And mine!" When all the candles were lighted we marched in a row from the shade of the magnolias to the wide walk of the Flower Garden.

Then came the fun! We marched in a row, holding our candles high above our heads, and as we marched we wound ourselves into a circle and then out again. Then we marched ten abreast, four abreast, six abreast, our candles held high and straight. Then we held our candles two and two in an arch, while the rest of us marched under the arch, and, stopping two and two, held their candles in an arch also, until a real triumphal arch of lighted candles was formed.

But the story must be told of the most exciting time when we lit our candles under the magnolias.

Grandmother's door had been shut tight for two days. All the house had been in tears yesterday, and to-day all the house seemed to be forcing back sobs, because Youngest Uncle, Grandmother's little boy, who seemed wonderfully big to us, with his six feet of height clad in gray, was reported in the slow-coming bulletins of war as "Missing." Why, we wondered, was he only "Missing" now when we had been missing him all the time? Such a fine playfellow he had been for us before he went marching away with all the rest of the men-people! Billy Button, our mothers' Black Mammy's boy, had gone with him, beating the drum. Now we heard that Billy was badly wounded, possibly dead, and Youngest Uncle "Missing."

From the gloom of the house, which we felt, but could scarcely comprehend, we had escaped to the shade of the magnolias and after our own manner were talking it over.

Judge and Doc were not with us. The negro boys had come, and after some mysterious whispering had carried them off. They stayed so long that we began to wonder whether we should report them as missing, too. But while we wondered we kept lighting our candles just because we had come to the four magnolias for that purpose in spite of the grief in the house, for we did not know what else to do, the grown people seeming for the time to have forgotten all about us. And while we filled our candlesticks we talked of the strange happening of these last days. Most of all we talked of the mystery of Grandmother's shut door. That door was always open to the sunlight and to a continual domestic processional. Indeed, the smallest of us ten grandchildren had merely heard, not seen, that the door was shut at night. We all dimly fancied that the shutting of that door made the darkness of the world, as if the sun itself was somehow shut in behind it, and as if morning and sunlight were let out to the earth by its opening. When our candles were all lighted, — we had lighted Doc's and Judge's unfinished ones for them, even though they were missing, — suddenly we heard a crackling in the hedge beyond the four magnolias, and there appeared Doc and Judge themselves. By their gestures they enjoined us to great silence, as they pointed down the grove path. Looking down there we saw Youngest Uncle approaching, Billy Button limping behind him !

After our hearty, though enforcedly quiet, greetings were over, we were told by Youngest Uncle that a surprise, even so joyous a surprise, might bring a serious shock to Grandmother. Then our thoughts turned again with awe to that closed door.

Youngest Uncle had learned from Doc and Judge, when the negro boys had brought them to him, that we were lighting our candles under the magnolias, and he had a fancy that we might best and most naturally bring him to Grandmother. He had learned that he had been reported missing. He knew, it seemed, that tears were shed and doors closed when one was — missing. It was later that we were to learn, by long talks together and by childish interpretations and piecing up of the words of our elders, how Youngest Uncle had been sent by a Higher Personage on a secret mission. How, in the chance of war, he had been reported missing. How the Great Personage himself had not known that the report was not

true. How he learned later that Youngest
Uncle had gloriously performed his mission and
had returned in safety. Then Youngest Uncle
had learned that Billy had been wounded.
All over the battle-field Youngest Uncle sought
the wounded boy, his body-servant, and, finding him, bore him off on his shoulders more
dead than alive. Now, after many dangers,
the two had reached home.

Since that most exciting day when we lit our
candles under the magnolias, many stories
have been written of the black body-servants
who carried their young masters off the field on
their shoulders; but the story we knew best
was how Youngest Uncle had carried Billy
Button on his shoulders from among the dead
and dying on the battle-field.

And now here they were, and the question
was how to present them to the household,
especially to Grandmother, without producing
a shock. With Youngest Uncle's advice we
decided to send the youngest grandchild to

tap at the closed door, to ask Grandmother to
open and to watch us at our lighted candle
play. We planned that the youngest grandchild should say that we promised "something good" at the end of our play if she would
promise not to be shocked. Close behind
the youngest grandchild we came, all of us
grandchildren in two rows, our lighted candles
held high in our hands, almost making a
triumphal arch, and Grandmother must have
divined what our "something good" was,
for no sooner had the youngest grandchild
spoken than the door was flung open wide
and down the vista of our flower candles
appeared Youngest Uncle, — but only for a
moment. For the next instant, it seemed to
us, he had, in long rushing steps, reached
Grandmother and clasped his arms about her.
In that instant all the grown-up people were all
at once laughing and crying about those two.
The news had reached the kitchen, and our
mothers' Black Mammy had rushed to the

scene, shouting, and now she was thanking God and beating her Billy Button over the shoulders with what Dilsey later told us were "love licks." From these she only desisted to hug Youngest Uncle about the knees and to bless him over and over for bringing back her "no-'count boy." On the outskirts of the excitement, we, all ten of us, shook our lighted candles wildly, and felt that we had borne a great part in bringing about so much happiness with so little shock.

CHAPTER XIV

GRANDMOTHER'S SPOOL OF PINK SILK

EVEN if it was War-time, we had birthdays, all ten of us. That is, all but Elise.

Elise had only one birthday in all War-time.

That was because she was a "leap-year-girl."

She could not have a birthday except on the twenty-ninth of February.

Wish as she might for birthdays, real birthdays, such as the rest of us had, she could have only pretend-ones, except when that one extra day in February came.

Elise said she never did love *pretends* of any sort, still less pretend birthdays, so she always just waited for the real day to come to celebrate.

We always called keeping our birthdays "celebrating." Every year we celebrated for

Judge, for Doc, for Amy, for Willy-boy, and
for Em, and for all the rest of us ten grandchildren, all except Elise.

Elise, as has been said, had to wait four
years to celebrate.

Then all at once she was four years older.

It was a great leap for her, she said, to grow
four years older all at once. She had only
made the leap twice. Once she had been all
at once four years old, then she had been all
at once eight years old. Now in War-time
she was to be all at once twelve years old.

It seemed to us all ten of us, grandchildren,
that we ought to do something most unusual
to celebrate for Elise on this third birthday
when she would be twelve years old.

But what could we do?

No toys had run the blockade for so long
a time that there were no gifts to be bought
in the shops of the neighboring town, even
had we had any money with which to buy
them. Our beautiful blue money (it was

beautiful money and still is — it can be seen now for sale, in old curio shops) had to be spent in hundreds of dollars to purchase the simplest things.

But neither great war nor small funds could prevent us from celebrating for Elise. So as the twenty-ninth of February drew near, we children often slipped away from Elise, going off in groups of two or three together, to plan how we were to celebrate for her.

"What is it you all talk of so much that you do not wish me to hear?" Elise often asked us.

The Aunts had told Elise that she must not expect anything in the way of a celebration on her birthday, because of the blockade. Our Aunts always told us the bare truth. Em once said that "Aunts, particularly Aunts who were not married, talked as bare boughs looked, while Mothers always talked as if there were at least some tips of flower-buds on the bare limbs."

But even Elise's mother had told her this time to remember that celebration was always more in the spirit, than in gifts.

So Elise had told us that if, *if* we did anything for her on this day upon which she would be, all at once, twelve years old, she would appreciate the spirit.

Doc said that the spirit was much harder to accomplish than gifts, even though toys had to run the blockade.

Judge said it took much more thinking to prepare the spirit.

So it was after much thinking on Judge's part, and much planning on Doc's that we decided to crown Elise: Queen of the Rare Day.

We were to declare ourselves to be her Loyal Subjects for all that day long. We were to obey her Lightest Behests that day. That last was the part that the next oldest grandchild, the one who was always poring over books, added to our plans.

Caro said she thought that we ought to tell Elise that part of the plan, for how was she to have Lightest Behests all of a sudden! Caro said Elise might wish to think over her Lightest Behests, just as we were thinking over our plans.   She might, Caro further suggested, even want to look them up in the dictionary!

But Judge said "No."   He said that people who had only one birthday in four years must be prepared for anything that might happen upon that day.   Elise must by nature be prepared to leap to conclusions.

So we chose a spot in our grandfather's woods, to which we had never been before. The next oldest grandchild said that there was much virtue in having our celebration in the virgin forest.   She said that meant a spot never before visited.   She said that she had noticed in all books, and in all of Grandmother's true stories of our Colonial and Revolutionary ancestors, that they did all the great things that they accomplished in or near the virgin forest. The boys chose a beautiful spot never before visited by us. There from the trees fell festoons of the wild muscadine, and these made the most delightful grapevine swings. To this spot the boys planned to roll the roundest and most beautiful pudding-stone that could be found. They found a suitable one, brown and thickly set with white and rose pebbles, as a brown Christmas pudding is set with all sorts of fruit. But the stone, when they found it, was so heavy that they had to ask Grandmother to lend them the negro boys and the newly broken calves to help them move the stone to the spot. When the stone was in our natural bower, we named it the Throne.

Then the boys spent many days carrying gravel, that is, round pebbles from the brook, with which to make a pavement about the stone. When many, many buckets of gravel had been brought and spread about the Throne, Doc said it was indeed fit for any Queen.

"With a carpet of gems," said the next oldest grandchild.

"Gems from the sea?" asked Caro.

"We might call it so," said the next oldest grandchild, "the brook is water anyhow, and all brooks run to the sea."

Then each planned to present Elise with an Emblem of Power. With this intent, how eagerly we watched the flower-beds in Grandmother's garden, for blooms in February were rare even in that rich old garden. Happily there were blooms for a golden crown. One of us made that of double yellow daffodils.

Then we cut a long bough from the Burning Bush that bordered the garden; the thorns were left on the bough, leafless still, though blossoming, and upon every thorn was stuck a different sort of early spring flower: hyacinth, rose, white, and blue; stars of Bethlehem; crocus; narcissus. Then we named that staff of many flowers, "Sceptre for Elise."

Then we made bouquets.

Then we made essays in flower emblems.
Aunts had taught us how to do that.

At last when the Day came it was cloudy.
Even Mothers said to us that it would do
just as well to celebrate on the next day.

But we knew that it would not.

Why, Elise had only one birthday in four
years! Of course after that long time, a half, a
third of a lifetime to most of us, no other day
but the real Day would do.

In the morning it spattered rain. We felt
as if all our work had been for nothing, and
it spattered a few tears, too! About midday
there was a sign of clearing up. We saw the
sun come out. We saw that there was enough
blue in the sky to make a Dutchman a pair of
trousers, so we knew that the rain was over.

Even Aunts said that we should be allowed
to go to our secret spot in the virgin forest
for our celebration.

So we went.

We had a grand celebration all to ourselves

(so we thought), and we were doing just as we pleased, which is the thing children love best to do, without observation or interference from the older people — when suddenly we heard a burst of laughter from behind a thicket of yucca.

"Fairies," breathed the next oldest grandchild.

"Witches," cried Caro.

"Aunts," declared Judge.

At first we were hurt and angry that we should have been secretly observed and laughed at when we were Making Obeisance and Presenting Homage and Obeying the Lightest Behests of our Queen of the Rare Day.

But Aunts came forward at once; we suspected they had, after all, but just arrived at the spot. They had Dilsey, Grandmother's own maid, with them, and Dilsey carried a great basket. Aunts had Dilsey carry the basket to the centre of the spot, then Aunts spread a feast for us. There were homemade cakes and candies and nuts from Grandfather's woods and plantation, and dried figs from Grandmother's orchard, for fruits from strange lands could no more run . the blockade than toys could.

"Aunts, you *are* bewitching," cried Caro.

"There is a birthday cake, a real large one," said Aunts, "which is to be cut in the long parlor when you come home from this frolic in the woods."

"Oh, Aunts, how lovely!" cried Elise. She had on her golden crown of daffodils, but it had slipped awry when she had leaped in fright from the throne at the sound of the laughter.

"With candles on it," said Aunts.

"Not candles!" cried Elise, waving her be-flowered sceptre in her joy and surprise.

"Twelve," said Aunts.

"Oh!" cried Elise.

We were burning only tallow candles then, for our candles had to be made at home, and wax was scarce.

"Pink cāndles," said Aunts.

"Pink?" breathed Elise.

It was wonderful. Whence could pink candles have come? We looked one at another, one at another, one at another, all ten of us, and in our look was the wonder: "Where could pink candles have come from?"

"Perhaps we have conquered the enemy," ventured the next oldest grandchild. For all lost goods and all things hoped for were to come, we thought, when we had "conquered the enemy."

Just at that moment the sound of horses' hoofs came to us, cantering down the road to the house. Aunts' faces grew as pink as the candles we were about to see, and they turned quickly and went to the house, not by the road, but through the woods, leaving us with our feast from our basket spread out on the ground. They left Dilsey with permission to wait on our wild-wood table, and Dilsey was as glad as she could be to help us with our celebration.

When, after our feast in the woods, we had
reached the house, we were not surprised to
find the Captain and the Lieutenant already
there, for we had, as has been said, heard the
beat of the hoofs of horses, and we knew that
only soldiers might have horses in those days.

As soon as we had reached home, our several
mothers and their several maids brushed our
hair, smoothed our dresses and ribbons, and
straightened the boys' collars and cravats, and
we were sent into the long parlor to cut
Elise's cake.   Aunts and the Captain and
the Lieutenant were already there.

The cake was large and white and beautiful.   The candles were indeed wonderfully
pink.   They were of wax, and they had been
tinted with pokeberry juice, we learned.   Uncle
Bee-Gum-Bob always saved some wax from
our hives, and, precious as it was now in War-
time, some of it had been used for moulding
the birthday candles.   Aunts had themselves
moulded those candles for a surprise.   They

had used for moulds the hollow cane cut from the cane-brakes on the creek banks; for candle-moulding was an art that ladies had learned and had taught to the house servants since War-times.

When Elise herself had lighted all the candles, we all stood around the cake sipping syllabub from Grandmother's great silver goblets, — then it seemed indeed to us that a most beautiful spirit hovered over the cake in the halo of light from the pink candles.

But the best was to come.

Dilsey, who had returned with us from the woods carrying the basket in which she had brought us the feast, now entered the long parlor bearing a silver tray, over which was spread a white napkin. She went to Elise, made her curtsy, and said: "Ole Miss say she wish you many happy returns."

Elise lifted the napkin.

Then we all saw on the silver tray the tiniest and most beautiful set of pink furniture.

Elise clasped her hands and cried out: "Oh, oh, oh!"

There were pink chairs, a pink sofa, a pink table, — just such chairs, sofa, and table as fairies might long for. The chairs were no larger than our own pink thumbs. The sofa was no larger than the Captain's thumb; we noticed that when he lifted it deftly to admire it. Elise could say nothing but Oh's, so great was her astonishment and pleasure. It looked as if those tiny pink and shining things must be the work of the fairies.

But it was our Grandmother who had made them.

Often since the years have passed it seems, in looking back, that Grandmother herself was as wonderful as a fairy queen — only different, quite different.

Grandmother had kept in her work-basket for so long, oh! since the War began, a spool of pink embroidery silk. She had once spoken of doing cross-stitch with it. She had also spoken once of doing briar-stitch with it.   But instead she had kept it just so until —.   It was Amy

"Aunts"

who was the first to think of that: "Grandmother's Spool of Pink Silk!" she cried.

Sure enough, the chairs, sofa, table all were made of pins upon which was wound and netted the pink embroidery silk from the spool. The work was smoothly and

stoutly done.   Not so long ago I saw the little set of furniture again.   Its roseate tints were faded, but it was still a treasure of a toy.

CHAPTER XV

OUR FOURTH O' JULY MINSTRELS

It was still War-time.

It had been War-time for a long time.

We were children then, and we did not know how long, but when we began to count birthdays since War-time it seemed to each of us that we could count at least *two* birthdays. Judge *thought* he could remember *three* that he had had since War-time.

It had been quite a while since any one of us had had a birthday, and we were beginning to wish that somebody would have one. Elise, as much as any of us, wished for somebody to have a birthday, but when we talked of birthdays, she shook her head and said: "You know how it is with me."

And we all, all ten of us, knew.

L 145

Even if it was War-time, there was always a birthday cake with candles on it, though in those days the candles had to be made at home. Sometimes Aunts and the house servants would let us help at the candle-moulding. The way we helped was to hold one end of the long homespun string that was to make the wick, while some grown person held the other end and twisted gently. Some of us were even large enough to know, not only how to hold, but also how to twist gently to the left. The grown person appeared to twist differently from us, though the grown person, too, had to twist to the left. Sometimes when we began to think of that we became quite puzzled, and being puzzled, we sometimes began to twist the other way. When we did that we were sure to get the whole of the wick tangled, and as soon as we did that we were told: "You are too little to wind wicks; go out and play!"

That made us feel sorry. When we had

been sent out to play, we often, instead of playing, sat under the camellia japonica hedge and talked of the puzzle of twisting. The oldest of the ten grandchildren said that she had found a way not to be sent off to play when she would rather twist. That was to just keep thinking: "Twist to the left" — not to think at all what the person at the other end was doing, only to think: "Twist to the left." But though the candle-moulding went on, no birthdays came. Then we went to Aunts and we asked them to count us all up, years and ages, and to tell us when the next birthday was coming. Then Aunts counted us all up, years and ages, but they said that no birthday was coming for any one of us for a long, long time. We were very sorry. But Aunts said: "Never mind. Something else is coming."

We asked: "What else?"

Aunts laughed and said: "The Fourth o' July."

We said that we did not know that the Fourth o' July came any more since War-time, and since we no longer celebrated the old Independence Day of the Union. Aunts said: "But it's coming this year."

Then Aunts said to us: "Bring us every day all the wish-bones that you find in the chicken at dinner at Children's Table."

Judge asked: "Aunts, why do you want so many pull-bones? One will tell which one of you will marry first."

"Never mind," said Aunts; "one is good, but we want many."

Then the Youngest Aunt said: "I vow I shall never marry first."

And Other Aunt said: "Nor I!"

It was all delightfully mysterious.

Every day as we sat at children's table we said one to another:—

"Do not forget to save the pull-bone!"

"Remember the wish-bone."

"Don't forget to save the merry-thought for Aunts."

For we called that one bone all those names. As we saved them we wondered how Aunts would ever marry if neither would marry first. Yet we dared not speak to them of our wonder for fear that again we might be called "Impertinent children!"

At last we carried all the wish-bones that we had saved to Aunts. Then Aunts said: "Bring no more merry-thoughts. Our work-baskets are like boneyards."

Just the day before the Fourth o' July, Aunts invited us to come at four o'clock to the long parlor. They said we should find something there. We wondered what that Something was.

That afternoon we put on our best dresses,— by that time even our best dresses were made of homespun cloth, dyed with wild-wood dyes. The boys brushed their hair; their heads were all wet and brushed very sleek, looking as they always did when we had company. And then we went into the long parlor, all ten of us in a row.

And what do you think we saw there? A large cake. It was iced as white as snow. And all around the cake stood ten funny bow-legged black men. All the little men had on red trousers, all had on queer little frock coats of black, all had queer little red hats. Two of the odd little men had tiny little cornstalk fiddles. Two had tiny flutes made of canes. Two had tiny gourds with tops cut off, and strung with silk threads as banjos are strung. Two had round gourds with tops cut off and covered with kid as drums are covered; two tiny drumsticks, each made with a match, were on top of the two tiny drums. Two had each a pair of wooden "bones" such as we often heard the negroes rattle in their plantation music. Oh, those little men were so funny! We ten grandchildren walked round and round the table that held the cake, and we laughed and laughed and laughed.

Then Aunts said: "These are the Merry-Thought Minstrels!"

Then we knew why Aunts had said: "Save all the wish-bones!"

For the minstrels were, all of them, wish-bones dressed in red trousers and black coats. On the love-knots a-top of the bones were put little black heads with white bead eyes and a stitch of red for the mouth. Aunts told each one of us to take one before the cake was cut, so each of us took a minstrel. Then Aunts said: "They are penwipers. You can wipe your goose-quill pens on the frock coats of the minstrels."

Then the oldest grandchild said: "Aunts, after all you did not pull any one of the merry-thoughts, so you do not know which one of you will marry first."

Then Aunts laughed and looked very rosy. And the Captain and the Lieutenant laughed, too. Then Youngest Aunt said: "I have told you I shall never marry first!"

And Other Aunt said: "Nor I!" That was to us very strange and very mysterious.

The next morning, as we were out at play, the maids and nurses were sent to call us in, and we were again dressed in our best clothes. When we met, all ten of us, dressed in our best, and on the way to the long parlor, we were told that there was to be a double wedding. We were so surprised that for an instant we could say nothing at all. It was Judge who, recovering from the shock of the surprise, spoke first. He said he thought it always did take two to make a wedding.

"Yes," said the grown folks to us; "but it takes four to make a double wedding."

Then all of us began to wonder "What four?"

The Rector from the town near by was already in the long parlor, and we were told to enter also. So we went, all ten in a row. And there we saw our two Aunts married to the Captain and the Lieutenant.

We were all ten of us very much surprised; and we were all ten of us very much pleased. Now we were never at a loss for something to talk about. For talk of the double wedding never ceased to be of interest. We talked of it even after the War was over.

THE following pages contain advertisements of a few of the Macmillan books on kindred subjects.

EVERYDAY ENGLISH

BOOK ONE

By

FRANKLIN T. BAKER
Professor of English in Teachers College and Supervisor of English
in the Horace Mann School

AND

ASHLEY H. THORNDIKE
Professor of English in Columbia University

This is the first book of

A NEW AND ORIGINAL SERIES OF LANGUAGE BOOKS

A HANDY, PRACTICAL, PERFECTLY
GRADED, AND BEAUTIFULLY IL-
LUSTRATED LANGUAGE BOOK FOR
THE FIFTH AND SIXTH GRADES

It treats language from a practical point of view rather than the technical.

Oral speech is treated first in each lesson.

In written speech letter writing is given fullest consideration.

Common errors of expression, both written and oral, are treated psychologically.

All formal instruction is based upon good literature.

The illustrations, many of them in color, are suggestive and inspirational.

Cloth, 12mo, xv + 240 pages, 40 cents *net*

THE MACMILLAN COMPANY

Publishers   64-66 Fifth Avenue   New York

The American School Readers

By KATHERINE F. OSWELL and C. B. GILBERT

A new basal series of school readers of unusually high literary quality
Cloth, 12mo

PRIMER $.30

This book is unique in that it is from the first lesson to the last a real story of real children, illustrated by photographs. It has a carefully chosen, limited vocabulary averaging about three words to a lesson. In addition to the continued story it contains more children's literature than most primers.

FIRST READER $.30

The primer children continue for a short space with new experiences. The greater part of the book is carefully selected and graded childlore.

SECOND READER $.35

All high grade literature, prose and poetry, adapted to second grade children, beautifully illustrated.

THIRD READER $.40

Children's literature with a vocabulary increasingly difficult, and with longer stories.

FOURTH READER $.45

A beautifully illustrated collection of high class literature, prose and poetry, chiefly in literary wholes. There are no scraps.

FIFTH READER $.50

Six hundred pages of literary wholes carefully graded, with notes and questions for appreciative study.

LITERARY READER $.00

An annotated and carefully edited collection of masterpieces suitable for study in higher grades and in rural schools.

THE MACMILLAN COMPANY

Publishers   64–66 Fifth Avenue   New York

The Gilbert Arithmetics

By C. H. GLEASON and C. B. GILBERT

BOOK I, $.36   BOOK II, $.40   BOOK III, $.45

These books are the latest product of recent careful studies on the subject of teaching mathematics to children.   They are unique in that they recognize both the scientific claims of the subject and the psychological claims of the student.

The present-day demands for a better arithmetic are summed up in the following four classifications : —

> I — Systematic and sufficient drills on the fundamental combinations to fix them in the memory beyond the power of loss.
>
> II — Clear and definite knowledge of essential principles, stated in simple language.
>
> III — A close relation between the arithmetic of the school and the problems of common life involving number, especially the problems familiar to children and appealing to them.
>
> IV — The scientific or inductive method of approach to new subjects, in order that the knowledge may be real as distinguished from verbal.

In the older arithmetics, the two first-named features predominated. These books were strong in drill and in formal statements.   They were weak in vital interest and in psychological approach.   Hence, the few who mastered them became exact and skilful ; but as the books lacked the essential qualities of interest and simplicity, the great majority of pupils wearied of the long, dry, and barren drills and failed to grasp the principles.

The newer books appeal more generally to the interest of children, and pay more attention to the inducing of principles.   But they tend too commonly to a disorderly arrangement, a disregard of necessary drill, and a lack of definitive statement.   Hence possibly, the frequent complaint of a lack of " thoroughness " or accuracy.

The Gilbert Arithmetics retain the virility and efficiency of the older arithmetics and offer as well the simplicity and attractiveness of the newer books.   But they are different from both old and new in certain essential respects.

THE MACMILLAN COMPANY

Publishers   64-66 Fifth Avenue   New York

The Everychild's Series

A new and unique series of supplementary readers for all school grades. The books will cover as nearly as may be the entire field of suitable literature, classified somewhat as follows:

FOLKLORE AND FAIRY STORIES
STORIES OF THE INDUSTRIES
GEOGRAPHIC STORIES
ORIGINAL STORIES RELATING TO CHILD LIFE
STANDARD AND CLASSICAL LITERATURE

The page is small, 3½ inches by 5½ inches, the type large and clear, making the books easy to read, thus meeting the demands of specialists in child's hygiene. The books will be handsomely illustrated, some in color.

To be published the coming spring:

Old Time Tales

Folklore stories for third or fourth grade, by KATE F. OSWELL, author of the American School Readers.

Nature Stories for First or Second Grades

By MARY GARDNER.

In Those Days

A true story of child life a hundred years ago, for fifth or sixth grade, by MRS. E B HALLOCK, beautifully illustrated in color.

Stories of Great Operas

By MILLICENT S. BENDER, the stories of six great German operas, taken from original sources in old German.

Nonsense Dialogues

Popular folklore in dialogue, for first grade, by MRS E E. K WARNER, author of Culture Readers, and other books

A Fairy Book for Second or Third Grade

By KATE F. OSWELL.

Stories Grandmother Told

Fairy and folklore stories for second or third grade, by KATE F. OSWELL.

Boy and Girl Heroes

Stories of child life of famous characters, by FLORENCE V. FARMER, author of " Nature Myths in Many Lands."

Historical Plays

Famous history stories put in dramatic form for reading, and also for acting by children of the higher, intermediate, or the grammar grades, by GRACE E. BIRD and MAUD STARLING.

Other books are in preparation.

THE MACMILLAN COMPANY
Publishers   64-66 Fifth Avenue   New York

CPSIA information can be obtained
at www.ICGtesting.com
Printed in the USA
BVHW04*0240290818
525927BV00008B/28/P